PUMPKIN EVERYTHING

BETH LABONTE

Copyright © 2018 by Beth Labonte

All rights reserved.

No part of this book may be reproduced in any form or by any electronic or mechanical means, including information storage and retrieval systems, without written permission from the author, except for the use of brief quotations in a book review.

❦ Created with Vellum

CHAPTER 1

"Grandpa's driven through Dunkin' Donuts!"

"So what?" I asked, crinkling my forehead as I walked to the refrigerator. My mother's hysterical tone wasn't quite matching up with the mundane words she spoke into the phone. Leave it to my mother to be overly dramatic about Grandpa going out for a coffee. If anyone had cause to be hysterical and dramatic, it was me. Cheating scumbag fiancé. Wedding canceled. Writing career hanging by a thread thanks to mega case of writer's block, thanks to cheating scumbag fiancé. It had been quite the chain reaction. But had she asked me about any of these tragedies recently? Nope. Here she was freaking out because Grandpa had utilized a drive-through window. I opened the fridge and pulled out a bottle of water. "Drive-throughs are a modern-day convenience, Mom. You might want to try one sometime."

"You're not getting it. He drove *through* a Dunkin' Donuts."

I froze midway through unscrewing the cap. "You don't mean...literally?"

"Yes, *literally*," said Mom. "Your grandfather has literally driven his Jeep through the front window of Dunkin' Donuts! It's probably all over the news! I just got a call from the Autumnboro police. I'm due on-air in ten minutes, Amy, and now I'm visibly shaken. Who wants to order cruise-wear from a person who looks visibly shaken?"

I walked back toward the couch with one hand clamped across my mouth. The police were involved? This was serious. "Is he okay?" I asked, sinking down into the cushions. "Was anyone hurt?" A vision of Grandpa, alone and scared in a courtroom, on trial for involuntary manslaughter, flashed through my mind. He didn't deserve to spend his last remaining years in prison.

"He's fractured his wrist," said Mom. "But nobody else was hurt. Thank God. He claims he was pressing the brake when the car just shot forward! Same old story they all use at that age when they forget which pedal is the accelerator." I could almost hear the eye roll in her voice. "I *knew* this would happen. I knew if I let him keep his driver's license that it was only a matter of time before disaster struck. I never should have left him alone up there."

"He's been up there alone for ten years, Mom. And he's been totally fine until just now." I slumped back into the couch, still processing my relief that Grandpa hadn't killed anybody. "Besides, he loves Autumnboro. You know it would crush him if you made him move."

Autumnboro, New Hampshire—the self-proclaimed Autumn Capital of the World—was bursting with pumpkins, mind-blowing fall foliage, and a population of just over five thousand. It was also the hometown I'd been successfully avoiding since escaping to Penn State ten years ago. A memory of soft green eyes, filled with the sort of sadness I couldn't even begin to understand, invaded my mind, followed by a familiar twang of guilt.

"It's inevitable, Amy," she said. "He's not getting any younger, and we can't keep dealing with these types of things if we're seven hours away. Plus, he didn't kill anybody this time, but next time..."

"Well, I doubt he's going to be driving again anytime soon."

"That's for sure. His Jeep was totaled, and I'm taking away his keys once and for all. For everybody's safety."

I frowned at the definitive tone in her voice...and at the trace of glee. Taking away his keys would eliminate a great deal of her Grandpa-induced stress, of which she'd been having quite a lot lately. Even with five hundred miles between us, our living arrangement with Grandpa had been running fairly smoothly. That was, until six months ago when he'd started calling Mom at all hours—confused about whether or not he'd taken his medication or panicked because he couldn't find his wallet. They were small things, but they'd put the idea in her head that he was getting too old to be living on his own, and now...Dunkin' Donuts.

I wanted him to be safe, of course. But, I also wasn't sure how he would survive on his own in New Hampshire without any wheels. I pictured him alone in his house, surrounded by empty pizza boxes and dead houseplants. Both his landline and his cell phone were dead for some reason, the lights flickering as a grandfather clock mournfully bonged each endless, passing hour. The howling of a lone coyote, his only connection with the outside world. I swallowed past the lump in my throat.

"So, are you taking some time off to go up there?" I asked. "He's probably going to need some help until his wrist is healed." My image of Grandpa surrounded by pizza boxes and dead houseplants was replaced by an image of him pathetically trying to unscrew lids from various jars—jelly, mayonnaise, pickle—as each one slipped from his hand and shattered into sharp, deadly shards on the floor. A barefooted Grandpa crunched down on them like Marv from *Home Alone*. I shuddered.

"You know I can't go up there," Mom said, indignantly. "They've got me working nonstop straight through Christmas.

I'm with Isaac Mizrahi every night this week, and they're flying Dennis Basso in on Saturday to showcase his new Christmas ornaments. Take time off? Pffft!"

I rolled my eyes as she scoffed loudly into the phone. She was always going on about Isaac Mizrahi. My mother hosted her own show on QVC—that's the home shopping channel headquartered down here in Pennsylvania—called *Sharyn's Closet*. She'd auditioned for the spot as soon as I'd accepted my admissions offer to Penn State, citing it as her secret, lifelong dream. Personally, I think her secret, lifelong dream was to get the heck out of Autumnboro as soon as I'd finished high school. Whatever the case, QVC booked her for the show, and she and Dad followed me south, leaving Grandpa alone up in New Hampshire. I saw a flash of those tragic green eyes again. Not Grandpa's. His were blue and merry and buried beneath two white puffs of eyebrows. The green ones weren't family, but they'd also been left behind—and the reason I'd gone, to be honest.

"So, what then?" I sighed, running my hand over the soft leather couch, suddenly wishing I had a nine-to-five office job, a husband, and kids. Anything to use as an excuse not to go up to Autumnboro myself. But I wrote horror novels from home—after college I'd become a bit of a self-published success story—and my cheating scumbag fiancé had moved out four months ago. Writer's block had settled in as soon as the wedding was canceled, meaning my days and nights were now filled by staring wide-eyed at stark white Word documents. I was alone, devoid of responsibilities, and at risk of developing chronic dry eye. But, still...I closed my dry eyes and waited for Mom's response.

"Well, it's a shame that nobody else from the family can go up there," she said.

"Mom, you know I can't—"

"I know, I know." She huffed. "You've been hiding down here for ten years. Why should I expect you to go and visit your poor, sick grandfather now?"

"He's not poor or sick, Mom. Merely maimed. And you know my leaving had nothing to do with him."

"I'm just going to have to hire a home health aide," she went on, ignoring me. "Even though, you know how he gets with strangers. You remember Greta, don't you?"

Greta was the housekeeper Mom had hired for him a few years back. As soon as he'd found out she was coming, Grandpa had hidden every potential valuable in the house beneath his mattress, which Greta found the first time she attempted to change the sheets.

"Of course, I remember Greta. And I *would* go, Mom, if only—"

"No, no," she interrupted. "He'll just have to deal with it. His wrist will be healed in a few weeks, anyway. And if the help *does* steal all his belongings, it'll just make the move that much easier on us."

"The move?" I furrowed my eyebrows. She'd always talked about moving Grandpa down here in an abstract sort of way. But this...this sounded certain.

"I've already looked into it, Amy. There's a nice assisted living facility right here in West Chester. He'd have his own room, three good meals a day, housekeeping..."

"Have *you* forgotten about Greta?"

She ignored me. "We'll have to notify the Parkers before putting the house on the market, but selling it will cover the cost of assisted living for quite a few years."

My stomach churned at the mention of the Parkers, and at the thought of selling our historic, two-family Victorian home. That house had been in our family for generations, and Grandpa had transferred ownership of it to my mother after Gram had died. It was in the most fantastic location, overlooking the town common, and the view from the turret during fall foliage season was like nothing else. Grandpa had grown up in that house, as had my mother and my uncle Pete—who now lived in Utah—and then me. The Parkers were our downstairs neighbors for as long as I could remember—Rebecca, her mother, and her two boys, Kit and Riley.

"I can probably take some time off during the New Year's clearance events," she continued. "Doreen or Jane can fill in for me. It's not like they need to waste their top talent selling the same junk nobody wanted last year!" She snickered into the phone, Grandpa's plight momentarily taking a backseat to her ginormous ego. "Anyway," she cleared her throat, "your father and I will go up there, pack up his things, maybe have a big yard sale..."

I pictured my mother sweeping coldly through the house like some sort of Wayne Szalinski packing machine—mechanical arms scooping Grandpa and a couple of his shirts into a box and mailing him off to an assisted living facility in a state he didn't know. I saw all his belongings spread out across the lawn, heartlessly slapped with neon yard sale price stickers, and it made my heart sink.

Poor Grandpa. He must have been so embarrassed, sitting there in his Jeep, half-in, half-out of Dunkin' Donuts, his wrist snapped like a twig and everybody staring. The poor guy probably didn't even get his chocolate glazed. And now suddenly everything was in jeopardy just because he'd made one tiny mistake. Gas instead of brake.

It could have happened to anybody.

"Wait," I said, another horribly depressing thought occurring to me. "What about Pumpkin Everything?"

When my grandmother passed away many years ago, Grandpa had taken over the operation of her beloved country store on Main Street.

Mom sighed. "We'll have to sell that, too, Amy. Grandpa only took it over because he thought Gram would haunt him if he let it go. But it's too much for him now. He's only been opening for a few hours a day, a few days a week. At this rate, I doubt he'll be able to keep up with the rent much longer. It's got to go."

It's got to go. There wasn't an ounce of nostalgia in her voice. Sure, we'd both left Autumnboro behind, but it had been a harder step for me. I'd loved growing up in that town, and I still dreamed about my view from the turret and the smell of autumn leaves as I walked across the common, kicking them up around my feet. Not Mom, though. Love for Autumnboro had clearly skipped a generation. I'd asked her once if she ever missed it and she'd replied with, *About as much as I miss my debilitating menstrual cramps.* Mom had had big city dreams. Big city dreams that were somehow fulfilled by hosting infomercials in the middle of Pennsylvania. But I couldn't fault her for that. The heart wants what the heart wants. But what about Grandpa's heart? It would crush him to not only have to leave his home but to sell the store that Gram had left in his care.

"But Pumpkin Everything is a landmark," I argued. "It's a fixture on Main Street! The town wouldn't even know what to do with itself if it closed!"

"Oh please. They sell scented candles not cures for cancer. I'm sure the town would manage. *Somehow.*"

"But it belongs in our family!" I cried, feeling panicky. "And so does that house." Through all the panic, the words sounded a bit hollow to my own ears. I hadn't been back to Autumnboro in a decade. Not even once. Mom and Dad drove up to New Hampshire to visit Grandpa a few times a year without me, and I saw him when he flew down to Pennsylvania for the holidays, but that was it. What right did I have to say such things?

Yet, I'd had my reasons for staying away.

After all these years, Kit Parker still lived in the downstairs unit, and I couldn't go back and face him. Not after the way I'd treated him during the most difficult time in his life, when he'd been at his most vulnerable. I saw those eyes and that pleading look of abandonment that had appeared right before I'd skipped town. That familiar twang of guilt rose again in my stomach, but this time it was coupled with a hearty dose of Grandpa-guilt. If I hadn't run off to Penn State, we would never have left him behind either. None of this would be happening right now.

"What do you want from me, huh?" asked Mom, her voice uncharacteristically gentle. "I finally have my dream career down here. Unless you're willing to pack your things and go up there—which you've made perfectly clear you are *not*—then I've run out of choices. The house and the store, they've always been the center of your grandparents' life, Amy. Not mine."

I wasn't sure how to respond. I glanced at my wedding dress, still hanging on the door to the hall closet. I hadn't let myself put it away yet. I'd actually *moved* it into the living room from the bedroom so I'd be forced to look at it more often. Some demented part of me felt that I deserved to stare at it, night after night, regretting the life choices that had led me to Pennsylvania and straight into the arms of my cheating scumbag ex-fiancé. If only I'd stayed with Kit…if only I'd tried a bit harder…yet, with all that regret, I'd never actually considered going back.

Unless you're willing to pack your things and go up there.

Was I? Was I finally willing? Before Grandpa had gunned it through a Dunkin' Donuts, my plan was to simply go on staring at blank Word documents, regretting my life choices, and waiting for it all to course correct into something tolerable. But now, things were happening very quickly. If I didn't move quickly too, Mom might sell everything out from under me—and with glee. But going back to Autumnboro? Yikes. As much as I loved growing up there, the thought of facing up to my past gave me the cold sweats.

"Well?" asked Mom, after I didn't reply for a good fifteen seconds. I was actually surprised she'd waited that long.

"Does Grandpa still do the scarecrows?"

"What?"

"You know, the scarecrows."

Every fall, after the first round of leaves had been raked into piles, Grandpa, Kit, Riley, and I would spend an entire weekend stuffing scarecrows. Grandpa provided bags of old clothing, hats, and shoes that he picked up from the local thrift shop, and the four of us sat outside in the crisp mountain air, drinking apple cider and hot chocolate, stuffing and sewing and turning it all into a motley cast of characters. We'd put the scarecrows on the front porch and all around the front yard—sitting them in wicker chairs, on railings, in the tire swing. It was quite the display. We even put some on the roof. People walking the town common would stop to take pictures, and every few years our house would end up in the newspaper. One year we even made it into the *Union Leader*.

"Oh, *that*," Mom said as if she were remembering a small-town murder scandal rather than my most treasured childhood memory. "Who would he still be doing that with?"

I shrugged. "I dunno. I always sort of hoped that he'd kept up the tradition with Kit and Riley, even as adults."

"That would be weird."

Right. Better that a scarecrow-less Grandpa sit alone in his empty pizza box-infested house until my mother drags him off to assisted living, severing my last connection to Autumnboro—and Kit Parker—forever than to be *weird.*

I stood and looked at myself in the mirror above the couch, twisting my hair up into a loose bun and letting it drop back down. My wedding dress was visible over my left shoulder, like a creepy, headless ghost bride from a horror film. Knowing what I had to do, I thought over the words I was about to say, and what they would ultimately mean for me. I swallowed down the resulting anxiety.

"I'll do it," I said, not quite loudly enough for her to actually hear.

"Excuse me?"

"I'll do it," I repeated with more confidence. "I'll pack my things, and I'll go up there, and I'll take care of Grandpa. I'll get him back on his feet and I'll check on the store. I'll make sure the house is safe and that he's taking his meds and whatever else you need. And maybe...maybe he won't need to move just yet. We don't need to rush into selling anything yet, right? Just...just let me see what I can do. Please?"

There was a long pause on the other end. Either she was contemplating what I'd said, or she'd passed out cold on the floor.

"How soon can you leave?" she asked at last, sounding a bit far away. She may have actually been flat on her back surrounded by QVC medics.

I told her I could be on the road the next morning, then hung up and sat on the couch for a long time, alternating between silently pondering what on Earth had just happened, and shouting rhetorical, swear-filled questions out into the universe. Still, I knew I had made the right choice. Maybe I would feel differently once I was pulling into Grandpa's driveway and Kit Parker was glaring at me from the front porch, but right now, I knew I couldn't abandon Grandpa in his time of need. I couldn't let my mother whisk him off to an assisted living facility, in another state, without at least trying to keep him in his own home. When I was young he'd always put my joy ahead of his own, and now it was my turn to return the favor.

CHAPTER 2

I never should have listened to Google Maps.

It meant well, I realize that. By directing me up the scenic route, it was trying to help me avoid a major traffic jam on the interstate. What it also helped me avoid, however, was any chance of rapid assistance should my car suddenly lurch forward like a cat with a hairball, clouds of smoke pouring out from beneath the hood. Google probably didn't even care what it had done to me. Just another dumb human to recalculate into an oblivion. *Moving on! Too-da-loo!*

I'd been sitting alone in the grass on the side of the road for forty-five minutes, only a few miles short of Autumnboro. I'd had enough cell phone reception to call AAA for help, but they were certainly taking their sweet time sending somebody out to get me. They were probably overloaded with calls from Google Maps victims. It was just as well. I'd been hoping to sneak stealthily into town via a deserted side street, so I wasn't exactly dying to get paraded down Main Street in a clunky old tow truck.

I kept glancing back into the woods, expecting a moose or bear to come ambling out. Autumnboro was pretty far up in New

Hampshire—right in the heart of the White Mountains—so it wasn't out of the question. At this time of year, they were probably stocking up on food, and what better food to grab than a defenseless hunk of meat just sitting there in the grass? Although, I couldn't recall anyone ever being eaten by a moose. Bears, sure. But bears didn't collect food for winter, did they? It would probably go bad while they were hibernating. It's not as if they sat around their caves salting meat like the Pilgrims.

I sighed as I watched the other cars zipping past. They were probably filled with sweater-clad leaf-peepers, happily bickering over radio stations and speed limits. Four short months ago, I thought that I, too, would be joining the ranks of the sweater-clad leaf-peepers, happily bickering with my husband—Orion Corcoran. I know, I should have realized way earlier than four months before the wedding that marrying someone with a name like Orion Corcoran couldn't possibly lead to anything good. But he was handsome, and athletic, and welp, here we are.

Even after all the years I'd lived in New Hampshire, I'd never been stranded alone on the side of a road before. I'd barely even had my driver's license before moving away for college. I took a deep breath and tried to force myself to think about something else. Someone else. I sounded like the intro to *Arrow*. *I must become someone else. I must become...something else.* That made me smile a bit, and I spent the next few minutes thinking about Oliver Queen, all suited up in a pair of tight black leather pants before my thoughts eventually drifted back to Kit Parker and my smile pretty much disintegrated. I'd already spent a good part of my seven-hour drive thinking about him and obsessively rehearsing what I would say when we finally met.

I plucked a dandelion out of the grass and rolled it between my fingers. We'd been a complicated thing, Kit and me. We'd had an idyllic boy-next-door, best-friends-to-romance type situation going on for years before everything changed, literally overnight. Kit's mother passed away suddenly from a heart attack the summer before our senior year. After that, he went so quickly from my funny, eternally optimistic boyfriend, to Kit Parker 2.0—a cold shadow of himself, filled with emotions that I couldn't begin to understand. I tried for months to bring him back around, thinking that my love should have been enough to help him fight through his depression. But it wasn't. The fact that I wasn't enough to make him happy was a tough pill to swallow for a seventeen-year-old girl.

As senior year went on, things only got worse. Kit's grades started dropping and he began cutting classes. He refused any sort of help from anybody and didn't want to talk about how he was feeling—even with me. And then, in January, when talk of the senior prom was just starting up, he told me that he wasn't going. He knew I'd been picking out dresses and planning for it for years. He knew I'd been planning to go to it with *him* for years. Yet, as I sat on his bed that dreary afternoon, staring at the back of his head as he tapped sullenly at his computer, he told me that he couldn't bring himself to suffer through it. *Suffer through it.* The words hurt, even now. After everything I'd put up with—his moods, his snarky remarks—he couldn't do this one thing for me. I'd hoped that after such a rough year, the senior prom might be a relief. That it might be one night for us to let loose and bring us closer again.

But he didn't think that he could suffer through it.

That had been the final straw. Such a shallow thing to be a final straw, in comparison to everything he'd been through—I knew that, and I hated myself for it—but I'd had enough, and I ended it. It was then, when I finally ended things between us, that I saw that flicker of emotion come back into his eyes. That desperate, pleading look of abandonment. A look that suggested that maybe, at zero hour, he did still feel something for me. But he said nothing. He let me go. The next day, I accepted my admissions offer from Penn State, a blessed seven hours away from Autumnboro.

My first semester, I met Orion—business major, lacrosse player, and obvious rebound guy—while the guilt I carried for breaking up with Kit continued eating away at me. Perhaps that was why I stayed with someone like Orion for so long. Had almost allowed myself to marry him.

At the sight of a tow truck slowly making its way up the breakdown lane, I dropped the dandelion on the grass and shot to my feet. Finally! I wrapped my arms tightly around my chest as the driver pulled the truck in front of my car, backed up a few feet, and rolled down the window. A pumpkin-headed scarecrow, holding a pair of jumper cables, was painted on the passenger door. *Autumnboro Towing*, it read beneath its splayed-out straw feet. That was our town mascot—a creepy scarecrow with a smiling pumpkin head and possibly murderous intentions. Autumnboro's answer to Mayor McCheese.

"Amy?" called out the driver, his eyes squinted. A note of recognition in his voice. "Amy Evangeline Fox?"

"Yes. That's me," I said, raking my fingers through my windblown hair. I didn't remember giving my über long middle name to the AAA lady. "Thank you for coming."

He stepped out of the truck, slammed the door, and walked around to meet me on the grass. I bit back a laugh as I took in his red buffalo check flannel shirt, puffy black vest, and jeans. Northern New Hampshire couldn't have sent a more generic ambassador. He was tall, with a short, scruffy beard, dark blond hair, and—

I sucked in my breath as I met his eyes. Not because they were a heart-stopping shade of molten chocolate, or a paralyzing, Edward Cullen shade of amber, but because they were a simple, soft shade of green that I'd been hoping to avoid at least until I'd managed to cross the town line. I mean, what were the odds? In a town of five thousand, quite good, I supposed. Crikey.

"Kit?" I breathed, squinting up at him against the backdrop of a brilliant blue autumn sky. He'd changed so much. The high school boy with the sweet face and the neatly kept dirty blond hair had been replaced by this more rugged, more lumberjacky model.

Kit Parker 3.0. Holy moly.

Pumpkin Everything
Copyright © 2018 by Beth Labonte

CHAPTER 3

"Hey, Ame," he said, tilting his head and giving me a cautious smile. "Long time, no see."

"Yeah," I said, weakly.

Yeah was definitely not one of the lines I had rehearsed on the ride up here. All the profound things I had envisioned myself shouting to him from the front lawn as he stood on Grandpa's front porch—or vice versa—had apparently gone out the window. As if to illustrate, a paper McDonald's bag came whizzing out of a passing car, nearly hitting me in the neck. Seriously? This was a national forest! Kit turned toward the car, arms in the air, as I picked up the bag and squeezed it in my hands.

"Some people," he said, shaking his head.

"Yeah," I said again. *Yeah* was all I had. It was confirmed. But then, despite the nerves and the sick feeling bubbling up in my stomach, I put the bag back down on the grass, walked right up to him and wrapped my arms around his neck. After a slight hesitation, I felt him squeeze me back. There was just something about the sight of him standing there—actually standing in front of me after all this time—that carried me forward on autopilot. I was like a starfish moving along the bottom of the sea—no brains, or mastery of the English language, required.

"I didn't even recognize you," I said, taking a step back and pulling myself together. "With the...with the beard." From the awkward *beard* motions I was making with my hands, you'd have thought he had an Abe Lincoln thing going on, rather than a teensy bit of scruff. But I liked it. Orion tried to grow a beard once and he looked like Ra's al Ghul. Not good.

"Yeah," he said running his hand down his chin. "I've been trying out a new look, going on...oh...eight years?"

"Ah," I said. "Right...long time, no see. Duh."

"Duh," he repeated with a small shrug.

We seemed to have left starfish mode and were heading into caveman speak. *Think, Amy...*

"So...you're a tow truck driver?" I asked, cringing at how horrible and judgmental I'd managed to make the words sound. There was nothing *wrong* with being a tow truck driver. The last I'd heard from Grandpa, Kit was working at a local ski and snowboard shop. And the Kit I'd known before that, well, he'd had other plans. Back in high school, the two of us would sometimes grab coffees at the Shaky Maple and go cruising down Route 3, looking at all the little motels left over from the 1950s and imagining how cool it would be to own one someday. We'd fix up all the rooms, making them super modern on the inside, while keeping the outside of the motel as retro as ever. I loved watching him talk as we drove, the sunshine pouring in through the sunroof making him almost godlike to my teenaged, lovesick self. He'd been considering going to college for hotel and travel administration up until his mom died. After that, he'd chosen to forego college in order to stick around for his little brother, Riley.

"I'm a tow truck driver," he confirmed, rubbing the back of his neck. "I was ready for a change of pace. And it's not a bad gig.

Sometimes you even pick a famous author up off the side of the road."

I batted a hand at him. "I'd hardly call myself *famous*."

"No, no....I meant Stephen King. He broke down here last week on his way back to Maine. Nice guy."

"Oh," I said, mortified. "Stephen King. Of course. Wow! I'd love to meet him."

We blinked at each other for a few seconds before Kit broke into a smile. "I was just kidding. Sorry. The most famous person I've picked up before today was the Autumnboro town clerk. But now, it's Amy Fox, *USA Today* bestselling author. How'd you do it?"

"I don't know." I shrugged. "Luck?"

"You've got some talent mixed in with that luck," he said. "I'm a big fan. I'm actually the only person in town who's read your books. But you didn't hear that from me. It's their loss. This town wouldn't know a good book if it climbed out of the Hellmouth and kidnapped the mayor."

"*Nightlife Negative*," I murmured, recognizing the opening scene of my debut novel. I'd written five more books after that one, proving myself more prolific than I'd thought possible, until my creativity crashed and burned alongside my pending nuptials.

"*Nightlife Negative*," Kit repeated. "Awesome stuff. Although *Bad Reception* was my favorite."

"Thanks," I said, smiling weakly.

He really had read my books. He wasn't just saying it to be nice. Had he recognized the town? Of *course,* he had. It didn't take a high IQ to realize that Fallsburg, Vermont was a thinly veiled version of Autumnboro, New Hampshire. Or that all its bumbling residents were based on people I'd known growing up.

The thing is, before I'd broken up with Orion, I never imagined a time that I would be back here, interacting with these people again. And after being away for so long, Autumnboro had sort of become as fictional to me as Fallsburg. But now...my stomach fluttered with nerves. This was a real town with real people living just beyond those trees. I took a deep breath. It would be okay. Kit said that nobody had read my books, right? I'd been published for years. Why should they suddenly start reading them now? It would all be fine. It would be good. It would be all fine and good and dandy.

"So," I said, clearing my throat, "I assume you've heard about my grandfather's accident?"

"Who do you think towed his Jeep out of Dunks?"

"Right," I said, cringing. "The tow truck driver."

"Speaking of," said Kit, clapping his hands together and pointing at me, "you probably called for a tow because you weren't enjoying standing around on the side of the road. Why don't you go wait in the truck? I'll get you hooked up, and we'll be out of here in no time."

"Sounds good," I said, picking the McDonald's bag up off the grass again and heading toward the truck. I climbed into the passenger side and shut the door, keeping an eye on Kit in the side mirror as he went to work. He looked so strange to me. I raised my eyebrows as he bent down to pick up a tool. Okay, so maybe *strange* wasn't the right word to describe him.

"And we're off," he said, jumping into the truck a few minutes later. His frame filled up a good portion of the driver's side. One hand gripped the wheel as we drove—large and a bit weathered, as all hands tend to be come fall in northern New England—and the other rested close to me, on the gearshift between us. As we drove along in silence, I watched the denim over his right thigh strain each time he pressed on the gas or brake.

"You know," he said, making me tear my eyes away from his thigh muscles, "I have a whole bunch of ideas for horror novels."

"Oh, yeah? You should've emailed me. I could've used the help. I'm in a bit of a slump."

"Email you book ideas? Like some stalker fanboy?"

"No," I said, laughing. "I would never think of you that way. I mean, unless I were Justin Timberlake. I wonder if he still has all your fan mail?"

Kit snorted. "I actually did think about emailing you," he said, declining to comment on his hard-core JT phase. "After I read your first book, I wanted to say something. I wanted you to know you had a fan who *knew you back when* and all that. But, you had Orpheus—"

"Orion," I mumbled.

"Orion," said Kit, with sarcastic emphasis. "Anyway, I figured if you wanted to be in touch, you knew where to find me." He glanced over, and I looked away as I fiddled nervously with the edge of my scarf.

"Did you mean it," I asked, letting the scarf drop and changing the subject. "When you said that nobody in town has read my books?"

"As far as I know. Why?" He looked at me, curiously.

"Just wondering."

He glanced at me again, a mischievous grin clearly struggling not to come out.

"What?"

"You're nervous."

"Why would I be nervous?"

He shrugged and looked back out the windshield. "If *I* had written an entire series of novels based on my hometown, and then found myself unexpectedly returning to said hometown, I might be a bit nervous." He shrugged again. "But, that's just me."

I put my head in my hands. "You know, then?"

"It wasn't exactly rocket science."

"Have you told anybody?" I asked, peeking up at him.

"Why would I do a thing like that?"

To punish me? To make sure everybody hated me if I ever came back to Autumnboro? It all sounded sort of ridiculous as the reasons played out in my head. But still...guilt.

"I don't know," I said. "You tell me."

Kit just shook his head. "Your secret's safe with me, Ame. But I do have one question."

"What's that?"

"How come *I'm* not in them?" He placed one hand over his chest.

"Are you serious?"

"I've identified plenty of people from this town, including our gym teacher, Mr. Marcoulier. Did I really mean less to you than Mr. Marcoulier?"

I just stared at him, my eyes wide. Out of everything that had happened between us, *this* was what he chose to confront me about first?

"Hey, I'm just teasing," he said, as he looked over and caught the horrid look on my face. "Seriously. I'm glad you didn't make me into a character. You probably would've turned me into some slimy embodiment of evil, hacked apart by the vengeful townsfolk. I should be thanking you."

"Speaking of slimy embodiments of evil," I said, "I'm glad you finally showed up to get me. I was imagining all sorts of gruesome scenarios if I were stuck on the side of the road any longer. Bears. Axe murderers. Bob. Ten years in Pennsylvania and you forget what it's like up here in the woods."

"No problem," said Kit, throwing me a friendly smile. "Maybe all you need to get out of that writing slump is a little vacation up here in the woods."

"Maybe. So, let's hear some of those book ideas. How far are we from town?"

"About five minutes," he said. "But I talk fast. So, I have this idea about a clown..."

CHAPTER 4

In the span of our five-minute ride, Kit rattled off at least ten terrible book ideas. Half of them were rip-offs of Stephen King novels. A quarter of them were rip-offs of *my* novels. The remaining quarter just didn't make much sense at all, though I didn't have the heart to tell him. Hearing the enthusiasm in his voice, and seeing the animation in his movements, brought me straight back to those drives along Route 3. The last time I'd seen him, he'd wandered so far from his natural state of cheerfulness that I hadn't been sure if he would ever come back.

"Oh, wow," I murmured, as we turned onto Main Street. It was early October, and Autumnboro hadn't dubbed itself the Autumn Capital of the World for nothing. Blazing red sugar maples lit up both sides of the street. By town decree, every store window had been outlined with garlands of colorful leaves and orange and white twinkle lights. Stacks of pumpkins and huge potted mums surrounded the base of each maple tree. Locals and tourists alike roamed the sidewalks dressed in cozy plaids and wooly scarves. The ones carrying Dunkin' Donuts cups and bags from Jed's General Store were easily discernible as the tourists. The locals leaned in doorways, chatting over cups from the

Shaky Maple. I rolled down the window and breathed in the crisp mountain air, along with a hint of apple cider.

Had it really been ten years?

I knew it was silly and self-centered, but I found it surreal that life had been going on in this town without me for an entire decade. The Obama administration had come and gone. And in that time, Kit, too, had been going on without me. But while he had changed immensely, the town hadn't changed a bit.

Kit slowed to a stop as we came upon Pumpkin Everything. Like all the other shops, the large front windows were outlined with twisted strands of orange and white twinkle lights. Inside the windows, wooden signs that read *Farm Fresh Pumpkins 25 cents* and *Grandma's Pumpkin Patch* were propped up on antique trunks, surrounded by jars of candles and teddy bears in cable-knit sweaters. I was pretty sure the window display hadn't been changed since Gram had passed away.

The sign on the front door was turned to Closed, and I noticed several tourists shaking their heads in disappointment before continuing on their way. Had they been able to go inside, they would have found antique bookshelves and hutches overflowing with pumpkin-themed merchandise—everything from scented candles and soaps to pumpkin-flavored coffee, candy, and pancake mix. It was a shame.

Although, to be totally honest, the thought of stepping inside that store and getting walloped in the face by such extreme levels of pumpkin spiciness made me feel a bit queasy. More than queasy, actually. My wedding was supposed to have been fall-themed. Growing up in New England, in a town called Autumnboro, it was only natural that I be all about apples and cinnamon and pumpkin spice lattes. But thanks to Orion Corcoran, and the twenty boxes of wasted fall-scented wedding decorations stinking up my condo, I'd developed a bit of an aversion. No, that's not true. I'd developed an extreme aversion. Like, the smell of pumpkin spice will literally make me ill. What kind of a man does that to a woman? I hadn't had time to explain this to my mother because a) I would have come off as a complete nutcase, and b) I couldn't leave Grandpa in the lurch, no matter my olfactory quirks.

"It's been closed a lot more often since the accident," said Kit, following my gaze to the store. "Are you guys thinking about selling?"

"My mom wants to," I said, with a sigh. "She wants to sell the house too, can you imagine? She wants to make Grandpa move down to Pennsylvania with us. That's why I came up, to help him get back on his feet. I don't want him to lose everything he has here." I looked over at Kit to find a rather odd expression on his face. "You okay?"

"Yeah," he said, quickly putting a smile on his face. "I think it's great what you're doing. Tom must be thrilled to have you back." He put the truck into drive and we started on our way down Main Street again. He took a left at the end of the street, rather than the right that would have taken us to the house. "I just need to make one quick stop before I drop you off."

We drove partway around the common and pulled into the parking lot of Goldwyn & Hays Funeral Home. Kit grabbed a paper bag off the floor of the backseat and went inside. While I waited, an older woman in a black skirt suit and a blonde bouffant came out the front door and stood there, staring at me from beneath the green-and-white-striped awning. I looked down at my phone and started scrolling through Facebook. *Back in the Autumn Capital of the World!* I posted from my author fan page, along with a photo I'd snapped of the town common. Within seconds somebody had commented, *When can we expect a new book???* I rolled my eyes. Before I could type out *Beats me!* or a poop emoji, a rap at my window made me jump. The old woman from under the awning was standing there making *crank-down-the-window* motions with her hand.

"Hiya."

"I know you," she said, pointing a long red fingernail through the window.

"You do?"

"I've seen your picture over at Tom's place. You're his granddaughter."

"Oh, yes," I said. "That's me. So...you know my grandfather?"

"I'm Maggie. I'm his *girlfriend*."

"Oh!" I said, stunned. Mom had never mentioned anything about Grandpa having a girlfriend. Although, with the transatlantic accent she was rocking, I could sort of see why he'd be into her. Grandpa loved the old movies. Mom must not have known, otherwise she'd have been all worked up about someone trying to steal her inheritance.

"Didn't know about me, didja?" asked Maggie, leaning her head almost fully into the truck. Crikey.

"No," I said, glancing toward the door, wishing Kit would hurry it up. What was he even doing in there? "I didn't. I'm sorry. Grandpa and I, we don't talk much. How, um, how long have you two been together?"

"One year and two months," she said, snaking her head back out of the window. "He's the light of my life."

"Aw, that's sweet," I said, my fear of this woman tapering off just a smidge. "I'm glad he has you, Maggie."

"And he's perfectly competent!" she suddenly shouted, taking a step away from the truck, raising one hand dramatically into the air.

"Excuse me?"

"I know how it goes! You have one little accident and suddenly the whole family's packing you up and declaring you incompetent!"

"No," I protested. "That's not why I'm here at all, I want to hel—"

"He hit the brakes and the car shot forward!" She continued to shout like some sort of television evangelist as she walked back toward the funeral home. "Shot forward, I tell you! It could've happened to anybody!"

Kit came out just as she was going back inside. I stared at him, wide-eyed, as he held the door for her and then climbed back into the truck.

"I see you've met Maggie," he said.

"*That's* my grandfather's girlfriend?"

"You didn't know?"

"He failed to mention her. Has she been retired from Hollywood long?"

Kit chuckled. "She's Peter Hays' widow. They still let her work here part-time, answering phones. She drove her car through an ATM a couple years back and her kids moved her into Winter's Eve Assisted Living. I think she's worried about the same thing happening to Tom. She knows his family lives four states away and she doesn't want to lose him."

That thought sort of made me sad. "What were you doing in there, anyway?" I asked, changing the subject. "Bringing lunch to your girlfriend, Morticia?"

"Girlfriend...brother...same thing."

"*Riley* works here?"

He shrugged. "Back in high school, after, um, you know...he became a little obsessed with death. He went through a whole Goth phase, went off to college, came back here, and decided he wanted to work at the funeral home. We all have our own way of dealing with things."

"But what does he *do* in there?" I asked, unable to picture little Riley Parker working all day with the corpses. "Does he handle the *bodies*?" I whispered the last word.

"Nah," said Kit. "Nothing like that. He's into advance planning. He helps people organize their funerals before they die. He loves it. Says he feels like he's giving people peace of mind."

I made a face. "He always was a little odd."

"You're telling me," Kit said as he put the truck into drive and we continued circling the common. "He's been super into Pokémon Go lately. He drives all over the state playing that stupid game."

"Funeral planning and Pokémon Go." I tilted my head from side to side. "I take back what I said. He's not odd. He might be the most interesting person I've ever met. You don't bring him lunch every day, do you?"

"Only when he forgets it."

I smiled as Kit rolled his eyes in exasperation. In the years since I'd been gone, he seemed to have taken on a motherly role to his younger brother. It was sweet, but it made me wonder if there was anybody around taking care of Kit.

"I didn't tell him you were back yet, by the way," he said, glancing over at me. "Although, I'm sure Maggie will fill him in. He'll be happy to see you again, Amy."

I just nodded. I wasn't so sure about that. I didn't even remember if I'd said goodbye to Riley before leaving for college. He'd been like the little brother I never had, and I'd just abandoned him without any explanation. At least Kit had known my reasons. But to Riley, I'd just vanished.

CHAPTER 5

The street around the common was called Poplar, and Grandpa's house was number six. We turned into the familiar, tree-lined driveway, and I fought back tears as I took it all in. For someone returning to their small hometown, the house still seemed enormous. Two twisted old oak trees stood grandly on either side of the brick walkway, one of them with a tire swing still hanging from its branches. The house was painted a light sky-blue with pale yellow trim, and an American flag flapped lazily from the huge front porch. I peered up to the turret that had once contained my writing room. It was actually just a spare sitting area with a wraparound bench and a few comfortable chairs. But when I was young, I would sit by the windows and stare out across the common, through the branches of those twisted old oaks, writing spooky stories in my notebooks.

After we parked, I jumped out of the truck and followed Kit around back to my car. We unloaded my things, and Kit unlocked the door to the house, letting us into the front hall. The stairs leading up to Grandpa's unit were straight ahead, and the door to Kit and Riley's unit was to my left. Ski jackets and winter coats hung—as they always had—from hooks along the back wall, and several pairs of skis and boots were piled into the corner. How many times had I gone up and down those stairs? Knocked on that door? Grabbed a coat off that hook? I tried to remember the very last time I'd done each of those things, but they'd been so routine that the memories were gone. Well, I certainly wouldn't forget the time I walked back into this house after ten years. I took a mental picture before heading up the stairs, Kit following behind.

About halfway up, I realized how steep the stairs were for Grandpa to be going up and down all by himself. Maybe I should look into getting one of those motorized stair lifts installed. I'm sure he wouldn't be thrilled about that. But if he wanted to stay here in his home, he was going to have to compromise on a few safety changes. Besides, they seemed sort of fun, didn't they? He could pretend he was riding the gondolas up Loon Mountain every time he came home.

Grandpa was currently at the senior center for the afternoon, so I unlocked the door to his apartment with the keys Mom had given me and was immediately bowled over by a pungent burst of cinnamon and pumpkin spice. I took a step back into the hall, bumping into Kit.

"What's wrong?"

I shook my head and tried not to inhale. Grandpa must have brought a few items home from the store. I couldn't confess my bizarre form of post traumatic stress disorder to Kit. I could hear him laughing already. Or worse yet, thinking that it served me right. That I deserved to be cheated on and suffer from bizarre neuro-nasal reactions.

"Just thought I was going to sneeze," I said, pulling myself together and walking back into the apartment. There, that was better. It was just the initial shock of it. I probably wouldn't even be able to smell anything after awhile, like those people who live with twenty cats or mountains of dirty diapers.

I put the bag I was carrying down on the floor and walked

further into the living room. While the rugs and curtains and furniture all looked the same, most other traces of my old life in this house had been replaced by White Mountains historical memorabilia. Grandpa had turned the living room into a virtual museum. From the same nails that had previously displayed Mom's generic scenic paintings, now hung framed black-and-white photographs of people in suits and hats and bustled skirts. The bookshelves to the left of the fireplace were filled with antique stereoscopes and stereoviews of local attractions. The shelves on the other side were filled with colorful memorabilia from Storyland, Six Gun City, Santa's Village, and Clark's Trading Post. A glass case across the room housed a display of antique lift tickets and ski memorabilia. On the wall above it hung a pair of wooden skis.

"Wow," I said, walking over to the front window. I crouched down to inspect the scale model of a Concord coach that was sitting on the deep sill. Grandpa had built it himself. It was painted pale yellow, and inside, resting on the velvet seat, were a tiny straw hat and a pair of lace gloves. "My grandfather really spread out, huh?"

"Hey, why not?" said Kit. "There's a lot of space here for one old man."

I bristled at what I thought he was implying. "What was I supposed to have done? *Not* gone away to college?"

"Whoa," said Kit. "What are you talking about?"

I stood up and fiddled with the drape cord. "You just made a dig at me because Grandpa's been here alone all these years."

Kit shook his head. "That wasn't a dig. I was just stating a fact. This is a big space for one guy. Even Riley and I have more room downstairs than we know what to do with. Anything else you think I was implying must've been your guilty conscience."

"I *would* have come back to visit," I pushed on, not quite ready to drop it. "If only..." I trailed off.

"If only what?"

"If...if Orion hadn't always been so busy," I said. "He couldn't take the time off to come up here. A weekend away could have cost him a million-dollar commission."

"You could've come alone."

"I don't like to travel alone."

Kit raised his eyebrows.

"Well it's different *now*," I said. "I had no choice this time. What does it even matter? I saw my grandfather on all the major holidays, I always sent him a birthday card, and my parents came up here *plenty*."

Kit held up his hands. "I never said you did anything wrong, Ame."

I looked intently into his face. How could he say that I'd done nothing wrong? I'd walked away from him when he was in the throes of a major depression, and I'd never even come back to check on him. I'd left my grandfather alone in this massive house like Edward Scissorhands. Why was he even being so kind to me? If I were him, I'd have left me to the hungry bears on the side of the road.

Unless, of course, I'd been wrong to think that he'd been hurt when I'd left. Maybe that look I'd seen in his eyes hadn't been abandonment. Maybe it was relief. Maybe my going off to a college seven hours away had been a blessing for him. No more of my stage-four clinginess and nagging to contend with. Somehow, over all these years, that thought had never occurred to me. *Maybe Kit was glad to see me go.* Now that I'd gone and thought it, my stomach didn't feel so good.

"I'm going to go get the rest of my stuff," I said quietly, turning and heading for the door. When I came back up, I found him standing inside Grandpa's hall closet, pointing to the ceiling. "Is that the attic access?"

"Um, yeah. Why?"

"Just curious." He stepped out of the closet and shut the door. Then he walked up to the wall separating the kitchen from the dining room and started knocking on it several times, in several different places. When he caught me staring, he tapped out "shave and a haircut," walked over to the couch, and flopped down into the corner. How many times had I curled up next to him on that couch, in that very same spot? I took a seat in Grandpa's recliner.

"Guilt trips aside," he said, lacing his fingers behind his head. "Don't you think Tom would be happier down in Pennsylvania, close to his family?"

I shrugged. "I'm sure he'd love being nearer to us, but look around." I motioned to Grandpa's makeshift museum. "Leaving the White Mountains would devastate him. This is the only home he's ever known. And do you really want my mother selling this house? Depending on who bought it, you and Riley might have to move out. And then..." *Then I'd never have any reason to come back here.*

"Riley and I can always find a new place to live," he said casually. Like it was no biggie. Like he was finding out he might need to move out of some crappy sublet. "Don't keep the house on our account."

"Just like that, huh? You'd find a new place to live, and oh well, whatever? Geez, apparently Grandpa and I are the only ones attached to this place."

Kit got that odd look on his face again, before tipping his chin toward the front door behind me. "Do you remember getting off the school bus in third grade? My mom would let me come up here, and we'd barrel through that door, dump our backpacks on the floor, and go straight for the TV."

"*Wrong.* We'd hit the kitchen first for pizza rolls."

"Right, right. Then it was *Are You Afraid of the Dark?* until dinner. No wonder you ended up writing horror."

"We were the coolest." I laughed.

"Giving up this house wouldn't be so easy for me, either." After a few moments of silence, Kit tapped his hand on the arm of the couch. "I don't want you to think that it would. It's just that sometimes we have to make hard choices. Sometimes we have to make sure that we're looking at the bigger picture."

"I appreciate the tip, Obi-Wan, but it's not happening. Not yet. Not ever. Not if I can help it."

The idea that maybe Kit hadn't been hurt at all, after I'd gone, flitted around my mind again. Maybe, instead of getting all philosophical about hard choices and bigger pictures, he should think about the fact that if he hadn't pushed me away, I never would have left. If it weren't for the way he'd treated me, Grandpa would still have his loving family around him, right here in his own home where he belonged. Assisted living would never have been on the table.

Then I remembered the reason why he'd treated me the way he had, and my stomach roiled with guilt. It wasn't his fault. His mother had been taken from him much too young. Rebecca Parker had always treated me as one of her own, happily tossing me in the car right along with Kit and Riley to go roller-skating, or sledding, or apple-picking. My memories of her were half the reason this house meant so much to me. Her death had torn all of us apart, but Kit in particular. Yes, he had hurt me. And yes, the result of that hurt led to our less-than-idyllic current situation. But none of it had been his fault. Not really.

I'd let myself forget that once, but never again.

CHAPTER 6

The senior center shuttle pulled into the driveway just as Kit and I came out the front door. I skipped down the front steps to meet Grandpa as the driver helped him slowly out of the bus. I frowned at the sight of his poor left wrist in a cast, reminding myself to stop by Dunkin' Donuts tomorrow to get him a treat. The fact that my car was dangling from the back of a tow truck meant that I'd be walking everywhere for a few days. Better me than him, though. Hopefully whatever was wrong with my car was an easy fix.

"Hello, hello!" said Grandpa, cheerfully, when he looked up and saw me standing there. "That's my granddaughter!" he said to the driver. Then he turned his head and shouted back into the bus, "That's my granddaughter!"

"Hello!" a chorus of wobbly voices echoed from inside. I waved blindly at the tinted windows.

"It's nice to meet you," said the driver. She was wearing a chunky hand-knit sweater covered in yellow and orange maple leaves. A nest of shoulder-length scarlet hair provided the missing autumn hue. "I'm Susan Blake. Tom's been so excited about having you back in Autumnboro! He's been talking all of our ears off!" She buddy-punched him in the shoulder, making him sway a bit. I stepped forward and threw my arm around him.

"It's nice to meet you, too," I said, shaking her hand with my free one. Susan didn't remember me, but I would recognize that hair anywhere. She'd been driving the senior center shuttle around town since I was in high school and had earned herself a starring role in my books as the Fallsburg town gossip. "I'm happy I could come," I said, giving Grandpa a little squeeze.

"Not many people would be able to put their lives on hold like this. Is your fiancé with you?" She looked over my shoulder toward the house where Kit was lounging on the porch swing. He waved. Apparently, Grandpa hadn't kept the senior center folks updated on the sad state of my love life.

"Well...."

"Tom told us you were getting married," she continued. "This *month*, come to think of it...but now you're *here*...so I'm not sure how you're going to..." She trailed off, her face dropping as understanding sank in. "*Oh*."

"Yeah..." I said, taking a side step toward the house, pulling Grandpa along with me. "It's kind of a long story. But it was nice meeting you, Susan." I turned and started hustling the both of us toward the house. I didn't feel like having my wretched story repeated to an entire busload of senior citizens.

"I've been meaning to read your books!" Susan shouted after us.

I stopped short, my eyes meeting Kit's. I narrowed them as he mouthed the words *uh-oh*.

"I'm gonna look you up as soon as I get home!"

I turned around to find that she had pulled out a notebook and pen. "Amy Fox. Is that with an *i* double *e* or the usual way?"

"A-M-Y," spelled out Grandpa. "F-O-X."

I stared at him, trying to telepathically get across the message to please shut his piehole, but it was no use. As Susan scribbled in her notepad, my eyes drifted from Grandpa's face, up to his bushy white hair. Large tufts stuck out from either side, and I mentally added *haircut* to my list of things we needed to do. Apparently keeping her fully competent boyfriend well-groomed wasn't on Maggie's to-do list.

Susan tucked away her notepad and pen, wriggling a set of scarlet nails at me as she stepped back up into the driver's seat. "It was lovely to meet you, Amy! Call me in the morning if you need a lift, Tom!"

As soon as the bus had driven off with a cheerful couple of toots, Grandpa turned and gave me a proper hug. "I'm so happy to see you, darling," he said, and my eyes filled with tears as I realized this was probably the first time in years that he hadn't come home to an empty house. I took him by the elbow and led him up the steps.

"Hey, Tom," said Kit, standing up, the swing swaying lazily behind him. "I had to rescue this one from the side of the road a few hours ago. Now you're both without wheels."

"What happened? Are you okay?" asked Grandpa, his brow crinkling with concern as he looked toward the tow truck. "An *Acura?*" He made a hoity-toity face that made me laugh.

"I'm *fine*," I said. "It was no big deal. The biggest shock was this one showing up to rescue me." I gave Kit a grateful smile. "Thanks for all your help, by the way."

"Don't mention it," he said, skipping past us down the steps. "Speaking of which, I've got to get that rat trap to the shop before Donnie goes home. I'll catch you two later." He paused halfway to the truck and turned around. "Hey, you didn't base any characters on Donnie, did you? As your biggest fan...I can't actually remember."

"Ummm...maybe?" I said, chewing on my lip.

Maybe my tuchas. In *Nightmare in the North*, a mechanic named Ronnie—known around Fallsburg for grossly overcharging his customers—sells his soul to an evil entity named Florg. In addition to overcharging everybody for brake pads, he eventually becomes a direct cause of their gruesome, bloody deaths. My stomach knotted as Kit solemnly shook his head, waved goodbye, and drove off. Donnie probably wasn't much of a reader, anyway. It would be all good. All fine. Dandy, even.

"He's a good kid," said Grandpa, as we watched Kit circle the common and disappear down Oak Street. "He checks on me every now and then. His brother, however," Grandpa made a face, "keeps trying to plan my funeral."

"That's his job, I hear. He says it gives people peace of mind."

Grandpa smirked. "You know what would give me peace of mind?"

"What?"

"Not thinking about my funeral every time that kid pulls into the driveway."

I patted him on the shoulder as we walked up the stairs and went inside. I helped him with his coat, gently wriggling it over his cast, and hung it from a hook by the front door.

"It's a sad state of affairs around here, darling. I drove through that donut shop like a fool. Now I've lost my car and my freedom in one fell swoop. And that was only Phase One. Phase Two is your mother shipping me off to some nursing home with the old people. Can I get you something to drink?" He shuffled off toward the kitchen.

"You're telling me those weren't old people out there in the senior shuttle?" I teased, following after him. I wasn't about to let my feeble grandfather fetch me a drink.

"Those people are doing their best to get out of the house and socialize. You're not old until your kids have thrown you in the slammer. Just ask Maggie."

"Speaking of Maggie," I said, shooing him out of the way and pouring us two glasses of iced tea. "I just met her outside the funeral home. She introduced herself and made it perfectly clear that you're *fully competent*." I said the words in my best Katharine Hepburn impersonation.

"That's my Mags," said Grandpa, giving me a thumbs-up.

"You know I'm here to help you stay in this house, right?" I asked as we took our drinks back out to the living room. "*Mags* seems to think I've come to pack you up and ship you out. But that's Mom's plan, not mine."

Grandpa placed his drink down on the coffee table and turned around to face me. "Don't take this the wrong way, darling," he said. "I'm thrilled that you've come. It's been difficult lately...and I know all about what happened between you and Aquarius—"

"Orion."

"Damn fool, that's what I've always called him. Sorry about that Susan, by the way. I didn't want to go blabbing your business to the town gossip. But what I'm trying to say is, what does a young girl like you want to come live up here in the middle of nowhere for? It's not exactly Cancun."

"Cancun?"

"You know," said Grandpa. "Young folks. Handsome fellas. Big muscles." He made *big muscle* motions with one hand.

I laughed and plopped down on the couch. "I don't know *what* you're talking about. Sit." I patted the cushion beside me, and Grandpa shuffled back over.

"I'm here because Mom might think you're some piece of furniture she can move around to wherever is convenient for her, but I don't. You have too many memories here. Too much love for this town. So do I." I glanced around the room, seeing ghosts of Kit and myself everywhere I looked. "You would have done anything for me when I was a kid. And now I want to do the same for you. Besides, I'm not going to be here forever. Once your wrist is healed, and you're back in your routine, I'm off to Cancun. Happy?"

"Ecstatic."

"Great. So don't you dare try to tell me that coming here was a mistake and that I'm wasting my youth in the middle of nowhere."

"Youth?" said Grandpa. "What are you, thirty? Thirty-one?"

"Twenty-eight," I said through gritted teeth.

"Ah. I suppose you've still got a few good years then." He patted me on the leg and heaved himself up off the couch. "Come on. I'll show you to your new room. Oddly enough, it looks a lot like your old room. The dust is free, but it'll cost you to use the john."

I laughed. "You're going to charge your own granddaughter to use the bathroom?"

"Business ain't what it used to be. Hope you packed some quarters."

CHAPTER 7

Grandpa left me alone in my old bedroom to unpack my things. My bed, with an unfamiliar comforter thrown across it, was still there, along with most of my old furniture. I walked over to the vanity by the window and sat down on the stool. Kit's mom had gone through a furniture restoration phase when we were young, and I'd watched, fascinated, as she sanded and repainted this banged-up vintage vanity that she'd dragged home from a flea market. Three days later, topped with a big pink bow, it had appeared in my bedroom. Rebecca had loved her two sons, but I think, in a way, I was the daughter she never had.

I stood and surveyed the rest of the room. Everything that I hadn't brought with me to college, Mom and Dad had eventually packed up and taken with them when they moved. The walls were empty, and my boots echoed loudly on the bare wood floor. As I opened the closet to hang up my clothes, my eyes were drawn downward to the initials AEF + KAP, written in purple Sharpie and surrounded by a red heart. I felt a flicker of teenaged embarrassment at the thought that Mom had seen it when she'd packed up my things.

I dropped to my knees so that I was closer to the words and thought back to the day they'd been written. Kit and I had just returned home from our sophomore year ski trip to Loon Mountain. We'd been seated side by side, all alone in a gondola, and even through our thick layers of ski clothes I could feel his warmth beside me. Things had been changing between us during those months leading up to the ski trip. I'd suddenly found myself drowning in self-consciousness every time he was in the room, aware of every single move I made whenever we were together. The tension was beyond thick in that gondola, and about halfway up the mountain he'd nudged me gently with his elbow. When I turned to look at him, he leaned in and kissed me. Gliding up that mountain at twelve miles per hour, my heart was beating fast enough to have propelled us way beyond the summit.

We'd said goodnight at the door to Kit's apartment that night —it had been so hard to tear ourselves apart—and I'd run straight upstairs to my room. I'd had this crazy, juvenile need to cement our new relationship in some sort of permanent way. Writing our initials on a piece of paper wasn't going to cut it, so I'd gone into my closet, pushed aside a stack of board games, and scrawled them on the wall in permanent marker. Then I'd pushed the games back into place and gone on with my day. I never considered that there might be a time when I no longer lived in that house, or when writing initials on a wall in permanent marker might not be enough to keep two people together.

I finished hanging my clothes and walked down the hall to check out the turret, frowning when I saw that my beloved writing room had been turned into a cluttered storage space. After getting Grandpa's permission to "knock myself out," I spent the next half hour dragging things out of the turret and into my bedroom closet, which had the added benefit of covering up those silly initials. The things I couldn't fit, I brought into Mom and Dad's old bedroom, which was empty, save for a rocking chair with one of Mom's old porcelain dolls seated on it—a sight I found both sad and completely terrifying.

After pulling most of the junk out of the turret, I found, under a pile of old clothes, the adorable antique school desk that Rebecca had fixed up for me and Kit. We'd used it to play school when we were super young. I pulled it into the center of the room and set my laptop on it. I pulled the white, wispy curtains aside and cracked open the windows. With the sound of rustling autumn leaves and the view of the mountains in the distance, I couldn't imagine a more ideal place to write.

Even if I wasn't staying in Autumnboro very long, maybe this would be enough to get the creative juices flowing again. I'd just have to be more careful this time. No more characters based on real-life people, no matter how irresistibly comical they may be. It shouldn't be too hard without Orion around to egg me on. He'd thought it was adorable that I'd come from such a small town full of backwater rubes. His words, not mine. Although, when it was my name that was printed across the book covers, that little detail didn't exactly matter.

The loud rapping of "shave and a haircut" on the front door made me jump. "I'll get it!" I shouted to Grandpa, happy to be of assistance.

"You know, you never do the two bits," I said, pulling the door open and finding Kit.

"Huh?"

"The jingle goes 'shave and a haircut, two bits.' Roger Rabbit would have exploded through the wall by now."

"That's because it's a call and response. I can't just do the *two bits* part by myself. Maybe *you* keep leaving *me* hanging."

Was that another subtle dig? Although the first dig, if Kit was to be believed, hadn't been a dig at all, but just my guilty conscience. Still, *maybe you keep leaving me hanging* was a loaded statement.

"Anyway," he continued before I could weave my neuroses

into a strand of coherent English, "I just came by to let you know your car is at the shop, and Donnie says he'll take a look at it tomorrow and give you a call."

"Great." I smiled. "Thank you. Again."

"No problem." He turned to go back downstairs, when he suddenly spun around, his eyes searching my face. "There is...one more thing."

"Oh?" My heart picked up the pace. Maybe that *had* been a dig, and now he was ready to talk. Ready to duke it all out. Ready to yell at me for having been such a mega teenaged super bi—

"When I dropped your car off, I told Donnie who it belonged to, and the name must have rung a bell..."

"Oh," I said, my stomach first dropping with disappointment, and then rolling over with impending doom. It was like obedience school in there.

"Yeah...he said he'd been meaning to read your books, he just hadn't had the time. But now that you're back in town..."

"Oh, no," I groaned.

"I couldn't stop him! He jumped on Amazon and ordered one right then and there."

"*Nightmare in the North?*"

"He didn't say." Kit shrugged. "Think positive, though. Maybe he'll find it so boring that he won't even make it past the first page."

"But Ronnie the mechanic is *on* the first page."

Kit whistled. "Tough break....sorry, Ame. Maybe I should've followed your lead and told him the car belonged to Jamie Rox? Ramy Cox?"

"Very funny." I rolled my eyes. "Don't worry about it. It's nobody's fault but my own if my car gets stripped for parts. Well, maybe Orion's."

"What's this about Oedipus?" asked Grandpa, appearing in the living room.

"*Orion*," I said. "And it was nothing. I'll see you later, Kit." I started to shut the door, but Grandpa stopped me.

"I was just about to order some pizza! Go get that grim reaper of a brother of yours and join us!"

Kit looked to me as if asking for my approval to stay.

"Sure." I shrugged. "You might want to warn Riley that I'm here, though."

"Will do," said Kit. "Thanks, Tom! I'll be right back."

I shut the door behind him and took a deep breath. Pizza with the whole gang. This was happening extremely fast. I hadn't even had a chance to figure out what I was going to say to Riley yet. Then again, maybe I never would. Maybe it was best just to get it over with. If Kit hadn't picked me up on the side of the road, I'd probably still be dreading my reunion with him, too. And so far, after all my years of avoidance and dread, it wasn't turning out half as badly as I'd imagined.

Then again, we hadn't actually discussed anything yet. And the night was young.

CHAPTER 8

Ten minutes later, Kit and Riley were both standing in the doorway—Kit with a bottle of red wine in his hand, Riley in a black hooded sweatshirt with the hood pulled up. The difference between the two of them was striking. Kit looked exactly like his mother, all lovely green eyes and dirty blond waves, while Riley had taken fully after their father. Earl Parker had taken off when the boys were very young—before they'd even moved into the house on Poplar Street—so I'd never actually met him, but I'd seen pictures when Kit and I flipped through his old family albums. Ten years older than the last time I'd seen him, and no longer a kid, Riley's resemblance to his dad was even stronger. Looking back at me from within that black hood was a pair of intense, wide-set brown eyes and an angular jaw. He pushed his hood back to reveal a mop of wavy dark hair swept up like a soft-serve chocolate ice cream cone.

"Hey, Riley," I said, stepping tentatively forward. "It's so great to see you again." I went right in for what turned out to be an extremely awkward hug.

"Hey," he said, patting me stiffly on the back. "Amy Fox. I literally thought we'd never see you again."

"That was before Grandpa *literally* drove through a Dunkin' Donuts," I joked, throwing Grandpa an apologetic smile that he did not return.

Riley just blinked, muttered something under his breath, and pushed past me into the house, pulling out his phone at the sound of an alert.

"Can you turn that thing off while we're here?" Kit called after him.

"There's a Jigglypuff around," he said cryptically, and disappeared into the kitchen. "I'll be done in a sec."

"Pokémon Go," explained Kit. "I told you, he's addicted."

"And he hates me."

"He doesn't hate you. You two just need to talk."

So do we, I thought, taking the bottle of wine from his hands. Not that I was dying for it to happen, but I was getting increasingly curious about what had gone on in his life after I'd left. Had he found someone else to support him in a way that I hadn't? When had he come out of his depression? Was he finally happy?

My stomach knotted at the thought of him having found happiness with somebody else. Or at the thought of him having been with somebody else at all. The feeling immediately turned into guilt. Of course, he had been with other women since I'd left. It was bad enough that I'd broken up with him right after he'd lost his mother. Did I really want him to have been lonely all this time? Of course not. I had gone so far as having almost gotten *married.* Maybe Kit wasn't so keen on that idea, either. Or maybe he couldn't care less. I still had no idea what he was thinking, and it was starting to put me on edge.

It would all come up eventually. It had to. And I had a feeling that when it did, Kit's sweet, cheerful façade would drop and the same coldness I was experiencing from Riley would come out. I knew that I deserved it, but I wasn't so sure I could handle it.

"Hey, Tom!" shouted Riley from the kitchen. "Have a change

of heart yet? I've got a great deal going on mahogany caskets. Spend eternity like a king!"

"No!" shouted Grandpa.

"Peace of mind, man."

"I'll give him a piece of my mind," muttered Grandpa, shaking his good fist in the air.

"Maggie says hello, by the way," said Riley, coming out of the kitchen and slipping his phone into his pocket. The Jigglypuff had apparently been secured. It hurt to see how friendly he could be to people who weren't me. "Said she's looking forward to movie night."

"Does Mom know about Maggie?" I asked, weaseling my way into their conversation.

"My love life is none of your mother's concern," said Grandpa.

"Yeah, but maybe if she knew you had a girlfriend, she wouldn't be so quick to move you down to Pennsylvania. Have you ever thought about that?"

"We're talking about your mother, right? Sells things on the TV? Three easy payments of nine ninety-nine? She'd have me down there twice as fast if she thought there might be competition for her inheritance."

That, of course, had been my initial reaction, as well. I just thought I ought to run the idea past him. Now that I knew we were on the same page, I let it drop. When the doorbell rang, I volunteered to run downstairs to get the pizzas.

"Amy Fox?" The delivery guy stared at my signature as I signed the credit card slip.

"That's me," I said, taking the stack of boxes from him. He looked vaguely familiar.

He took a step back and looked up at the house as if suddenly realizing where he was. "You're Tom's granddaughter?"

"Yes," I said. "I'm visiting for a bit. You know him?"

He tucked his pen back behind his ear. "Sure do. I deliver here at least once a week. Tell him I said hello, would you?"

I knew it. Grandpa would have been alone and surrounded by empty pizza boxes if I hadn't come back. I mean, he was still going to be surrounded by empty pizza boxes, but he wouldn't be alone, and that was the main thing.

"Of course," I said. "Thanks for the grub." I was closing the door when he started talking again.

"Tom always mentions some books you wrote?" he said. "Like, you're famous?"

"Oh, that," I said, reluctantly opening the door again. "I'm not really famous. You know how grandparents tend to exaggerate..."

"No, no. Tom's a straightforward guy. If he says you're famous, I'm going to take his word for it. And now that I've met you, I definitely have to get one of your books! I've already got your autograph!" He dangled the yellow credit card slip in the air. Great. I knew I should've paid cash.

"Awesome," I said, shifting the boxes as they started burning my hands. "Thanks again. Bye." I nudged the door shut with my foot and walked back upstairs. Awesome, indeed. This was starting to get out of hand. At least I hadn't poked fun at the Autumnboro House of Pizza in any of my books.

"The delivery guy says hello," I told Grandpa, putting the boxes down on the kitchen table and grabbing a stack of paper plates from the pantry. "He also says he's going to buy one of my books—and possibly sell my credit card receipt on eBay."

"That must've been Mike," said Grandpa. "Nice kid. Great bowler, too."

I froze with my hand on the stack of plates. "Bowler?"

"Sure. He's been playing with the Autumnboro Ballers for years."

I closed my eyes. While the House of Pizza had escaped mention in my books, the Autumnboro Ballers most definitely had not. I looked over my shoulder to find Kit fighting back a laugh. Why, oh why, did I have to portray them as such over-the-top nerds? I actually really liked the guys from the bowling league. Rebecca used to take the three of us to the lanes once in a while where we'd see them practicing. They had cool jackets and were always giving each other high-fives. Never mind the fact that they got to eat hot dogs and pretzels like three nights a week.

I tried to push Mike out of my mind while we ate. It wasn't difficult as Kit and Grandpa quickly turned the conversation to town gossip. Ninety-year-old Ed Woodbury had put up a ten-foot fence, spray-painted with hideous neon graffiti, in order to discourage anybody from purchasing the five-thousand-square-foot home that had been built on the edge of his property. The police had been out there to talk to him, but since he had a permit for a fence, there wasn't much anybody could do. Kyle "Moose" Moriarty—owner of Moose's Mini Mart, who'd earned his nickname thirty years ago driving straight between the legs of a moose during his road test with the DMV—was considering expanding his store after the White Mountain Reiki Center had gone out of business.

"I could've told them that would happen a *long* time ago," said Grandpa. "Reiki. Who needs it? Whatever it is. Did anybody think to ask *me*?"

And so it went.

Riley, who'd been artfully avoiding eye contact with me for the entire meal, didn't contribute much to the conversation. Mostly, I just snuck glances at Kit as we ate, discreetly making note of all his mannerisms and jokes, trying to tell if he was truly and genuinely happy. He seemed to be. But outward appearances can be deceiving, and I needed to be sure.

After the plates and pizza boxes were cleared away, Grandpa moved into the living room and turned on the TV. *Sharyn's Closet* was on, and he quickly drifted off to sleep. Riley excused himself, leaving with as much of a goodbye to me as I had given him ten years ago. Kit and I listened to the sound of the front door opening and closing, then looked out the window to watch him jog across the street to the town common, head down, staring at his phone. Off to find another Jigglypuff.

"It's a nice night," Kit said once we were alone. "Care to join me on the porch?"

"Sure." The glass of wine I'd drank with dinner had helped ease some of my nerves, which also meant that the questions I had were bubbling up and very close to spilling out. Was this the right time? I wasn't sure. But as I poured myself a second glass of wine, put on my puffy black coat, and followed him outside, I figured that I was about to find out.

CHAPTER 9

Kit flipped on the orange and white Christmas lights that had been wound around the porch railing, as well as a small space heater sitting between the two rockers.

"It's been a long day," I said, sitting down and inhaling deeply. I had a moment of total bliss as the mountain air and earthy smell of crunchy leaves hit my lungs. It was pure autumn, and I took it all in without a trace of wedding-related nausea for the first time in months. Then Kit lit a pumpkin spice candle on the table between us and my stomach turned over.

"You okay?" he asked.

"Yeah," I said, zipping my coat up to my chin and burying my nose in the collar. "Why?"

"You look like you smelled a dead animal. The same thing happened when we went upstairs earlier."

I lifted my nose out of my coat, deciding that I may as well come clean. "It's just things that smell like that," I tipped my head to the candle, "have been bothering me for a few months now."

"Like an allergy?"

I shook my head, rocking slowly in the chair. "My wedding

was supposed to have been fall-themed. You know, hay bales, pumpkin centerpieces, the whole clichéd shebang? The kind of wedding Autumnboro high school girls dream about." I paused. When I'd been an Autumnboro high school girl, dreaming about my wedding day, it hadn't been Orion I'd been envisioning. "Anyway," I continued, "I'd been in the middle of crafting pumpkin centerpieces and assorted cinnamon-scented tchotchke when everything went south. Now I've got boxes of the stuff that I can't seem to part with, my apartment reeks, and all those smells do now is remind me of how everything went wrong."

"Ouch. Shall I blow it out?"

The candle was pretty, flickering between us in the darkness. "No. I need to get over it. It's getting sort of ridiculous. Besides, once the initial pungency passes, I'm okay."

"Smart move coming back to the most autumn-smellingest town in the country, by the way."

I laughed. "Autumn-*smellingest*?"

"I'm not the wordsmith." He smiled before taking a sip of the beer he'd brought outside. "So, tell me, Amy, because I got zero details out of your grandfather, what exactly happened between you and Origami?"

"*Orion*." A snort escaped. "And he was cheating on me. For years. Although, I only figured it out four months before the wedding. And he was kind of a jerk...also for years."

"What'd you stay with him for, if he was a jerk?"

"Dunno." I shrugged. "I guess I didn't know it could be better than that."

When I looked over at him, I could see the hurt in his eyes. Of course I'd known that it could be better than that. Even at his lowest point, Kit had been so much better than that. And now, he probably thought that I'd forgotten, or that I'd never appreciated him at all. *I didn't know it could be better* just seemed like the natural thing to say when asked why you stayed in a lousy relationship. It was certainly the safest thing to say. Unless I wanted to admit that I'd stayed with Orion because I'd been racked with guilt and hadn't felt like I'd deserved better, which seemed a bit much for a casual chat on my first night back.

"Anyway," I said, crushing a leaf to bits with the heel of my boot. "You know all about my atrocious love life. Got anything juicy to spill about yours?"

Kit rested his left elbow on the back of his chair and angled himself toward me. "Nothing juicy, sorry. I was with someone for four years, but that ended pretty undramatically a while back."

"Oh, yeah?" So there *had* been someone else. My stomach knotted as I pictured this obviously ravishing woman, swooping in and holding his hand while they visited Rebecca's grave. Whoever she was, she was nurturing and sympathetic and didn't even *want* to attend her senior prom, let alone break up with someone over it.

"Yeah," said Kit. "She ended up moving to California. She couldn't take the winters up here. She asked me to go with her, but I wasn't ready to leave. I'm still not." He reached back and lovingly ran his hand down the strip of yellow trim behind us. "She wasn't right for me, anyway."

The super-woman image I'd dreamed up faded away as I studied his face and fought the urge to reach out and touch his cheek. Resisting the desire to feel the scruff of that beard against my fingers, so different now from what he had felt like in high school. At the thought of us having been that close, pleasant memories began drifting back to me. Memories of sitting on this very same porch, talking until late into the night. Memories of sneaking into his bedroom, which was directly below mine, even later in the night. The scent of the candle between us was starting to become tolerable.

"Why wasn't she right for you?" I asked, taking a sip of wine and shivering as a breeze blew across the porch.

Kit turned the space heater up a notch and shrugged. "A lot of reasons. She was always trying to change me. She couldn't understand why I wanted to stay here. Why I never wanted to leave the house I grew up in when she couldn't get out of hers fast enough."

"I'm sorry," I said, reading the sad expression on his face. "I didn't mean to dredge up painful memories for you."

"It's okay. I asked you first, anyway. It's human nature to want to know if the one that got away ever got away with somebody else."

The one that got away. Was that what he was to me? He hadn't gotten away like some determined fish struggling free from a net, emerging triumphantly into open water. No, I'd dumped him out. Weak and with a broken fin, I'd dumped him out into the ocean, over the petty offense of not wanting to take me to the prom, not knowing or caring if he would make it on his own. How could he be the one that got away, when I'd let him go?

"Is this weird?" I asked. "Us sitting here, chatting about our failed relationships?"

The corner of his mouth hitched up into a crooked smile. "It's a little weird. But good weird. I think."

Good weird? Better than bad weird, I supposed, which pretty much had no potential for a positive spin.

"I'll take good weird," I said, gently kicking him in the calf with the toe of my boot. "I didn't mean it, by the way, when I said I didn't know it could be better than Orion." I looked over at him and straight into his eyes. "You were."

He held my gaze, reached out his beer bottle, and clinked it against my wineglass. Clinking glasses was so far from the reaction I'd been expecting, but just like *good weird,* I'd take it.

"So, how's your gran?" I asked, changing the subject. "Still loving Florida?"

"She is," he said. "She's been down there almost five years now. She's really into pickleball and beach tennis. Who knew?"

"I can see that." I nodded slowly. "She was always a hot ticket, that Iris."

Kit smiled. "So, when's the next book coming out?"

I sighed and relaxed back into the rocker. "Honestly? I have no idea. I haven't written anything in months. I should have had a first draft done by now."

"Big deal. Give yourself a break."

"It *is* a big deal!" My voice came out louder than I intended. "Stephen King writes a book in a weekend," I continued, lowering my volume.

"Where'd you hear that one?"

"The Internet."

Kit stood and walked to the front door. "Come on inside. I want to show you something."

Riley still hadn't returned yet, and the thought of being alone inside with Kit gave me a little boost of nervous excitement. Not that we hadn't been alone outside on the porch all evening. But being alone *in there*, with the door clicking shut behind us, and the mystery of what he wanted to show me hanging in the air... I stifled a giggle, blew out the candle and followed him in.

The apartment looked majorly different than the last time I'd been inside. After Iris moved to Florida, Kit and Riley had removed most of her classic country décor. Sweatshirts and jackets were strewn around the couches and chairs, and two video game controllers sat on the coffee table beside a huge box of Goldfish crackers. The television was mounted on the wall opposite the couch, flanked on either side by two built-in bookcases. The one on the left still housed Rebecca's huge collection of books.

Those books had been my first taste of sci-fi, fantasy, and horror, and I smiled as I walked up to them, scanning the titles. When we were kids, Kit and I would pull them down at random, giggling as we flipped through looking for swear words and dirty bits. As we got older, I started borrowing them to read and had long, insightful discussions with Rebecca.

Kit came up alongside me, scanning the shelves until he'd

found what he was looking for. He pulled down a copy of Stephen King's *It*, and flipped to the end.

"Discover a new swear word?" I teased.

Kit smiled but shook his head. "Look...started September 9, 1981. Completed December 28, 1985. Four years. Here's another one." He put *It* back on the shelf and pulled out *The Stand.* "February 1975 to December 1988. Thirteen years, Amy. Thirteen *years*. Shall I keep going?"

"Okay, I get it!" I laughed. "Maybe I shouldn't get my facts from Internet memes. Although, *The Stand* is like a thousand pages long, and my bank account is slightly smaller than Mr. King's." I walked away from the bookcase and over to the one on the other side of the TV. Those shelves were more sparsely filled, containing more framed photographs, board games, and movies than books. I ran my finger along the spines of the few that sat on the bottom shelf. All seven *Harry Potters. The Hunger Games. The Lord of the Rings. Flipping Houses for Dummies*. I stopped at the last one and looked over at Kit.

"Have you guys been flipping houses?"

"We gave it a shot," he said. "But it was too much work with our day jobs, and it didn't make us a ton of money. We learned a lot about renovations and construction, though. Made some good contacts that might come in handy someday."

"Do you remember our drives down Route 3?" I asked. "Checking out the motels?"

"Of course. I still go sometimes."

"Seriously?"

"Seriously. Once in a while, one of them goes up for sale and I imagine all the possibilities...color TV, air-conditioning..."

"Free Wi-Fi?"

"Let's not go too crazy."

I laughed. "You should totally buy one and make that dream a reality. It would be awesome. Kit's Motel. The Parker Lodge. I would definitely stay there."

"Would you?" That mischievous gleam was back in his eyes, making me feel a little weak in the knees.

"Well, as long as you had free Wi-Fi." I tore myself away from his eyes to glance up at the clock—an antique in the shape of the Old Man of the Mountain—and realized how late it was getting.

"I should probably head back up there," I said, pointing to the ceiling through which I could hear Grandpa faintly snoring. "It's probably up to me to make sure he gets into bed and everything. Brushes...er....takes *out* his teeth?"

"Tom has false teeth?"

I shrugged. "I knew there'd be a learning curve."

"He's happy to have you here, you know?" said Kit, walking me to the door. "He lights right up when he looks at you. I noticed during dinner."

"I'm glad," I said. "I just hope it's not too hard on him when I leave again."

"Yeah," said Kit. And then after a pause, "Me, too."

CHAPTER 10

Me, too. What had that meant?

I'd set my alarm for bright and early the next morning and was standing in the hall outside Grandpa's bedroom, replaying my conversation with Kit over and over in my head. I hadn't thought to ask Grandpa if he needed help with showering or getting dressed, so I was listening intently for any sound to indicate that he was awake. I needn't have worried. When his alarm clock finally went off, it rivaled the alarm bells of the Autumnboro Fire Department. It wouldn't even be much of an exaggeration to suggest that several firefighters had jumped into their trucks and driven halfway down Main Street, sirens blaring, before realizing it was just my grandfather sliding out of bed again. When the bells ceased their clanging, I knocked gently on the door.

"Gramps, you up?"

Silence. A moment later, the door cracked open and a sliver of Grandpa appeared.

"You're not going to check on me every morning to make sure I'm alive, are you? That's what they do at the assisted living. They have this key to all the rooms, and they jiggle the knob really loudly as they come in, trying to wake you up. Trying to see if you're dead. You take too long to say hello and they send you to the morgue."

"That's morbid," I said, trying not to laugh. "And *no,* that's not why I'm here. I was just checking to see if you needed any help showering, or getting dressed, or whatever." I waved my hand in the air as if I could perform it all with a magic spell.

"And blind my granddaughter on her first day here? I don't think so." He tried to slam the door in my face, but I stopped him, pushing it all the way open.

"How do you shower with that thing?" I pointed to his cast.

"I'm supposed to wrap it in a plastic bag and seal it with duct tape. Maggie helped me do it the last time."

"Which was?"

There was a pause while he did the calculations. Never a good sign when it comes to personal hygiene. "A few days ago…give or take." From the state of his hair, it had clearly been more give than take.

"Hold on." I ran into the kitchen and grabbed a plastic grocery store bag and a roll of duct tape. Then I went to work wrapping up his cast.

"Thank you, darling," he said. "I'll take it from here."

"Are you sure?" I asked. "I can help you in the shower. I mean, not *in* the shower. I could maybe stand outside the shower and—" And what? I had absolutely no idea. I cleared my throat. "Do you maybe have some sort of a long brush?"

Grandpa, looking understandably offended, shook his head before walking past me into the bathroom and locking the door.

"I'll just get started on breakfast then!" I shouted through the closed door. That should be less traumatic for the both of us.

"Sausage and eggs?" he shouted back.

"You got it!"

Mission in hand, I went into the kitchen and began clearing dirty pans off the stove. I spent ten minutes scrubbing a frying pan before I thought to check for the actual food. Just because Grandpa requested sausage and eggs didn't necessarily mean he had sausage and eggs. With a sinking feeling I opened the refrigerator. No eggs. I scanned the kitchen counters. Three different kinds of Oreos, but no bread. The odds were definitely not looking good for sausage. I checked the freezer and found a pint of coffee ice cream and a bag of frozen peas wrapped in a towel.

I hated to disappoint him on my first morning here, but I didn't even have a car to run out and get anything. I suppose I could walk to Moose's Mini Mart, but it was freezing outside so early. Living in a two-family home did leave me one other option. I threw a sweatshirt on over my pajamas, ran downstairs, and rang the doorbell. Showing up at Kit's apartment, begging for scraps with bedhead and morning breath hadn't exactly been at the top of my to-do list. It was, however, a straight-up testament to the love I had for my grandfather.

"Hidy-ho, neighbor," said Kit, smiling as he opened the door, and sending my stomach into a cloud of butterflies. He was pretty much the opposite of me—fresh and clean out of the shower, hair still damp. I could even detect a hint of minty toothpaste from his freshly-brushed teeth. All his layers of flannel shirts and North Face vests that I'd seen him in yesterday had been stripped down to jeans and a snug white tee. I took a few steps back before speaking.

"Morning," I said, raking my hands through my nest of hair. "I'm sorry to bother you so early."

"Not a problem," said Kit. "What's up?"

"Well, I sort of promised my grandfather that I'd make breakfast before realizing that we don't actually have any food. You wouldn't have a couple of eggs I could borrow? And maybe a few slices of bread? And, um," I cleared my throat, "some butter?"

He paused for a moment, probably asking himself whether or not I was for real, before motioning for me to follow. "Come on in."

"Sorry," I said again, trailing him into the kitchen. "I'll pay you back."

"Don't worry about it." He opened the refrigerator and handed me an entire carton of eggs and a stick of butter. Then he grabbed a loaf of bread off the counter and a box of frozen sausages from the freezer, piling them into my arms.

"Are you sure?" I asked. "I only needed like four slices."

"It's fine." He opened a drawer next to the fridge and pulled out a spare key. "Put back whatever you don't use when you're done."

"I really appreciate it," I said, pocketing the key. "I'll have to run over to Moose's later to get some stuff. Literally run, since I'm carless."

Kit made a face. "You can't grocery shop at Moose's."

"Like I said, no car."

"But all they have at Moose's is cookies and ice cream."

"That helps explain the contents of my grandfather's kitchen."

"I get off work at four thirty," he said. "I'll drive you guys to an actual grocery store so you can stock up. I would've offered to take Tom sooner if I'd known. I feel bad that I haven't done a better job of checking on him."

"It wasn't your job to check on him," I said, making my way back to the front door. "Besides, he would've just shooed you away. He wouldn't let me anywhere near his shower."

"Slightly different, don't you think?"

"I suppose." I laughed. "So, you're serious about taking us to the grocery store?" Picking me up off the side of the road had been nice, but he'd only been doing his job. Schlepping me and my grandfather to a grocery store was a whole other level of kindness. "I can always set him up with a PeaPod account or something. I probably should anyway, for when I go back to Pennsylvania."

"Let me save you the delivery charge this one time," he said. "There'll be plenty of time for PeaPod after you're gone."

"Right." I tried to ignore how morbid he made that sound. Living with Riley, that sort of thing probably went right over his head. "Thanks, Kit. I'll see you tonight then."

Fifteen minutes later, I had a pan full of scrambled eggs, sausages crackling on the back burner, and a piping hot stack of buttered toast. I was pouring Grandpa a cup of black coffee when he walked in, trying to shove his bagged wrist through the cuff of his sweater.

"Let me help you with that." I exchanged my spatula for a pair of scissors and carefully cut off the bag, helping him wriggle his sleeve down over his cast. I pulled out a chair for him then brought all the plates over along with a glass of water and a small cup containing his morning pills. Not bad for my first day.

"So it begins," he muttered, eyeing the pill cup.

"What do you mean *so it begins*?" I narrowed my eyes. "You're supposed to be taking these every morning. You've been taking them, right?"

"Of course," he said, popping them into his mouth. "Mmmm, pills."

I stared at him until he swallowed. "I'm buying you one of those weekly pill organizer things. No more forgetting." Not that I was surprised his pill taking was inconsistent. His medicine cabinet was a total mess. I'd gone through it last night after he'd gone to bed, trying to figure out what he was currently taking and at what time of day to give it to him. Luckily, Mom had given me a copy of his current medication list. I'd never have been able to figure it out otherwise. Many of the medications had expired years ago, including a half-empty bottle of Viagra. Some things you can never un-see.

"You know, if you forget to take your pills and another disaster happens to occur, Mom's going to ship you out of here faster than you can say Boston cream donut."

Grandpa dug moodily into his eggs, but he didn't respond.

"I'm here to keep that from happening," I added.

"I know," he said, finally looking up at me. "And I appreciate that. I appreciate this breakfast, too. You know, I didn't even think I had any food around here."

"You *didn't*. I had to borrow from Kit. I sacrificed my pride for you, old man."

At the mention of Kit's name, Grandpa looked at me with his bushy white eyebrows raised. "Oh, yeah? You've already been down there to see him?"

"What's that supposed to mean?"

"You two used to be a thing, weren't you?"

"Um, yeah, we used to be a *thing*," I said, a bit thrown. "Back in high school. Many moons ago."

"So, what happened?"

I paused with my fork halfway into a piece of sausage. How was it possible that Grandpa didn't know what had happened? Our two families had shared this house for years, borrowing shovels and lawn mowers, babysitting each other's children, sharing a front porch and a backyard. It was with a jolt that I realized I'd never actually told my grandfather why I'd chosen to go to Penn State, a decision that resulted in his whole family leaving him behind. If I'd even thought about it at all back then, I'd probably assumed that my mother would fill him in. Which she clearly hadn't. He probably thought I'd gone for the academics.

So I told him everything. He'd already known, to an extent, about Kit's depression after his mom died, and how he'd had some trouble in school our senior year. What he hadn't known was how Kit had pushed me further and further away, refusing to admit that there was anything wrong. He hadn't known about Kit refusing to take me to the prom, or about how that had been the final straw. He hadn't known—and this realization sort of killed me—that the real reason I'd been afraid to come back here all these years had nothing to do with him, and everything to do with facing up to Kit.

"So that's why you stayed with that Odysseus for so long," Grandpa said when I had finished.

"*Orion*. And I'm not sure what you mean," I said, knowing exactly what he meant.

"I mean, you almost married that fool because you were trying to punish yourself for how you treated this one." He jerked his thumb toward the door.

Hearing the truth from someone else—and hearing it stated like such an obvious fact—made something twist inside my stomach. I pushed my chair back and started briskly clearing away the plates. "Are we ready to go?"

My plan for the day was for us to walk into town and open Pumpkin Everything. I figured I could check out the inventory, locate any unpaid bills, and see about hiring somebody part-time. I knew Grandpa wasn't crazy about the idea of hiring an employee—Gram had always run the store on her own—and he had his stubborn pride. But I'd convinced him to let me duct-tape a plastic bag around his wrist, so there was some hope for him yet.

CHAPTER 11

Half an hour later, I was placing my hand over my nose as Grandpa unlocked the door to Pumpkin Everything. I braced myself for the blast of pumpkin spice.

"You okay?"

"Fine," I said, lowering my hand. I couldn't keep letting stupid Orion Corcoran ruin the scent of my hometown. And I certainly couldn't let him ruin my ability to help my grandfather get his store back into shape. Besides, this had been the scent of my childhood, and a million pleasant memories, long before it was the scent of my canceled wedding and garbage relationship. Mind over matter. "Maybe we could just..." I propped the door open with a large rock that had been painted like a pumpkin, letting some fresh air cycle through. It couldn't hurt.

The wooden floorboards creaked in all the old, familiar places as I followed Grandpa into the store. The rustic bookshelves and hutches were still there against the walls, draped in their burlap and lace doilies, and overflowing with pumpkin everything. The floors were crowded with display tables and wooden barrels filled with stuffed animals and kitchen gadgets and cedar-scented sachets. A few feet below the ceiling, a shelf ran around the perimeter of the store displaying vintage New Hampshire signs and souvenirs. These were part of Grandpa's collection and weren't for sale. Two long wooden tables sat end-to-end in the center of the store, covered in maple sugar products and jars of old-fashioned stick candy.

I smiled and grabbed a stick of root beer flavor. Kit and I had eaten boatloads of these candies as kids, always assuming they were free of charge to the owner's granddaughter. Grandpa gave me some serious side-eye as I peeled back the wrapper and popped it in my mouth.

"I'll pay you back," I promised.

"I'll add it to your tab."

We spent the next few hours unpacking the inventory that had been delivered after Grandpa's accident and going over store operations. I was surprised to find that he had moved into the twenty-first century and was using a computer for almost everything. He'd made a Pumpkin Everything Facebook page and ordered almost all of his inventory online. He was even using accounting software to handle the finances.

"This is great," I said, honestly impressed. "I was thinking maybe you were still using big, old Ben Franklin-style ledgers and hadn't restocked the shelves in ten years. But everything is so organized and modern! There's no way we can let Mom sell this place. Not yet."

"I do still enjoy it here," he agreed. "But, it would be nice to be able to come in whenever I felt like it, rather than having the whole dog and pony show depending on me. I'm too old to be here seven days a week." He shrugged. "But what else can I do?"

"Um, you can hire a part-time employee," I said. "That's what you can do. Can I at least put a sign in the window? See who turns up?"

"Don't take this the wrong way, darling. You're my granddaughter, and I love you. I'm just not so sure you're the best judge of character."

I let my jaw drop. "What's *that* supposed to mean?"

"Need I bring up that fool, Archimedes, again?"

"*Orion*. And fine. Point taken. I promise not to hire anybody without your approval. Deal?"

"If I get to heaven and find out your grandmother was displeased, I'm sending her down to haunt you."

"Perfect." I stuck out my hand, and he shook on the deal. "I love a good ghost story."

Not long after I'd posted a Help Wanted sign in the window, a young blonde woman wandered in looking slightly disoriented. She was carrying a cardboard tray full of coffees and wearing a somewhat familiar, blue crocheted top.

"Tom?" she shouted as the door swung shut behind her.

"Can I help—"

"Josie?" I was cut off by Grandpa's voice resonating from the back room.

"Tom?" She breezed right past me, following the sound of Grandpa's disembodied voice.

"Josie!" Grandpa emerged from the storage room, arms outstretched, a piece of stray packing tape dangling from his elbow. He gave her a hug and helped himself to one of the coffees from the tray before turning to me. "Amy, this is my good friend Josie. She brings me coffee and keeps me company! Josie, this is my granddaughter, Amy."

Grandpa had a Maggie *and* a Josie? Who knew?

"It's nice to meet you," I said, shaking her hand and trying not to stare. Looking at Josie head-on was like looking into a mirror. Same hair color, same brown eyes. And I suddenly realized why that sweater seemed so familiar. "Is that from *Sharyn's Closet?*" I asked, gesturing to her top.

She glanced down as if to remind herself what she was wearing. "Oh, yes, it is! As soon as I found out that Sharyn was Tom's daughter, I started ordering everything from her show! Now whenever I stop by, he says I remind him of his family."

Ouch. Poor Grandpa. Whether he realized it or not, he'd befriended a woman who looked just like me and managed to dress her up in Mom's clothes. I'm going to assume, for my own mental welfare, that it was all on a subconscious level.

"I've been so worried!" she said, turning back to Grandpa. "I heard about your accident, and then when the store was closed, I started thinking the worst. I knew you'd been in the hospital—and sure, it was only for a few hours—but with flu season gearing up you never know what you might contract. They say the very old and the very young are at highest risk." She gave Grandpa a pointed look.

"Well, I wouldn't say I'm *that* young," said Grandpa, with a chuckle. "But, no, no, aside from my wounded pride and a broken wrist, I'm perfectly fine. Although, I'll tell you, Josie, I stepped on that brake pedal and the car shot forward!" He shook his head and threw his good hand out to the side. "But does anyone believe an old man?"

"Well, I believe you," said Josie. "That sort of thing happens to me *all* the time. At least once a week. Sometimes once a day!"

"You step on the gas instead of the brake once...once a day?" I asked, slowly.

"Sometimes I think a little fairy comes in and switches the pedals around while I sleep!" She shrugged while Grandpa nodded along in earnest agreement, as if pedal-swapping fairies were a totally reasonable theory. Yikes. "Oh, I've been so rude!" she continued, remembering the tray of coffees she'd placed on the counter. "Would you like one? I always bring four because I never know what this one's going to want. I've got your classic PSL, a cappuccino, a green tea chai latte, and Tom just grabbed the black, so you're out of luck there."

"A cappuccino's great," I said. "Let me pay you back."

She snorted and looked at Grandpa, then they both started laughing.

"What's so funny?"

"Josie's loaded," said Grandpa. "She won the Powerball."

"Powerball?" My eyes bugged out of my head. Powerball jackpots were typically nine figures. "That's amazing! May I ask how much?"

"Oh, hundreds of millions," she said nonchalantly. "You know, you think having money is going to change your life, and it does...a bit." She tossed her long, platinum waves behind her shoulder. "You're able to hand out coffee everywhere you go, and buy every item on QVC, and everybody suddenly loves you and wants to be your friend." She leaned back against the counter, looking dreamily up at the ceiling. "I bought my parents a house on Cape Cod and my sister a lovely one up in Maine. And I bought one for myself right here on the river, with a pool and a spa and a panoramic view. But in the end, it's still just me rattling around in there. And eventually you realize that very few people actually *want* to be your friend." She smiled at Grandpa.

"Have you done any traveling?" I asked, not expecting to feel so sympathetic toward someone who was rolling in that kind of dough. But Josie seemed sweet, and lonely.

"Oh, no. I've got a terrible fear of flying," she said. "And of traveling. Hodophobia, it's called. That's the travel one, not the flying one. The flying one is called aerophobia. And don't even get me started on the possibility of travel diarrhea. It's all very unfortunate for someone in my financial situation." She whispered the words *diarrhea* and *financial situation*, though I wasn't sure why. We were the only three people in the store, and she'd already told me without hesitation that she had hundreds of millions in the bank.

"You should come and work here!" exclaimed Grandpa, out of nowhere. I shot him a look. For someone unsure about hiring outside help, he sure was taking the initiative.

"Grandpa, why would she want to work he—"

"*Could I?*" cut in Josie, sounding—and this is merely a guess—

more excited than when she'd won Powerball. "You wouldn't even have to pay me!"

"You really want to work here?" I asked.

"Not work, volunteer!" She walked toward the center of the store, twirling around, narrowly missing a jar of watermelon stick candy. "I'm here all the time anyway. I would love to help out!" She batted her eyes at Grandpa, and he slapped a hand down on the counter.

"It's settled! Welcome aboard!"

Josie clasped her hands in front of her chest. "Can I start today? Right now?"

"Sure," I said, as Grandpa nodded enthusiastically. "We were just unpacking some boxes out back. Come on, we'll show you."

I had to admit that her enthusiasm was contagious. As odd as it seemed that she wanted to work here for free, what did I know about being a millionaire? Rich people were allowed to get bored like the rest of us. Maybe even more so. I mean, look at Christian Grey.

"This is so amazing," she breathed, following us into the storage room and looking around as if she'd just awoken in Oz. "And don't you guys worry. Lunch is on me today."

CHAPTER 12

At three o'clock, we turned the sign on the door to CLOSED, locked up, and waved goodbye to Josie. Walking home with Grandpa was a slow endeavor but allowed me the time to really look around and appreciate my surroundings. Growing up in Autumnboro, I'd always taken it for granted that our town was surrounded by so much natural beauty. Looking up at the mountains now, it was hard for me to believe that such a stunning sight could have ever faded into the background.

"Josie seems nice," I said as we passed The Plaid Apple diner and prepared to cross the street to the common. "Maggie's not jealous, is she?" I nudged him gently with my elbow so he'd know I was kidding.

"No, no," he chuckled. "Josie's like a granddaughter to me."

"Ah...maybe *I* should be the jealous one then," I joked. Sort of.

"Poppycock," said Grandpa, as we stepped into the crosswalk, my hand in the crook of his arm. "You're one of a kind."

I smiled and squeezed his arm, feeling a bit better. Yet, I still couldn't shake the idea that Grandpa had been missing us.

Missing *me*. How had such a basic concept escaped me all these years? Had I truly been that self-centered?

"Oh, I forgot to tell you," I said once we'd arrived back home and were taking off our coats. "Kit's offered to take us grocery shopping tonight."

Grandpa settled into his recliner and turned on the TV. *Sharyn's Closet* had already started. "Go ahead without me."

"Don't you want to pick out what you want for food?" I asked, a flicker of panic arising in my gut.

"I trust you."

"Oh. Uh, okay. I should be back in time to make a late dinner."

"Have dinner out," he said, waving me away. "Go ahead."

"What about you?"

He wiggled his fingers in the air. "My button-pushers are still in working order. I'll order out again. You can cook me the Beef Wellington tomorrow."

I reluctantly agreed and headed off to my room. I'd been counting on Grandpa being there as a buffer between me and Kit should any awkwardness set in as we cruised the cereal aisle. But it looked like I was on my own. I'd come all the way up to New Hampshire to help the old man sort out his life, and what does he do? Leaves me in the lurch. Geez. I opened the closet, sighed, and surveyed the meager selection of clothes I'd brought with me. I didn't *really* need to change. The jeans and sweater I'd worn to the store were perfectly presentable, and the odds were good that I wasn't even going to be removing my coat. Then again, now that a dinner might be involved, and it would only be the two of us...

I pulled a dark gray tunic sweater from the closet and a pair of black leggings from the dresser. Then, as if on autopilot, I went into the bathroom, totally redid my makeup, curled my hair, and spritzed myself with an ancient bottle of Fantasy by Britney Spears that I found beneath the sink. At the sound of "shave and a haircut" at the front door, I switched off the bathroom light and walked into the living room. Grandpa sniffed the air.

"What?" I asked, throwing him a look.

He just raised an eyebrow and went back to watching Mom on TV.

I opened the door, immediately remorseful as I took in the sight of Kit standing there in his tow truck driver's outfit of jeans and a flannel shirt. Not that he didn't look good—I had a feeling that Kit 3.0 would look amazing in a flour sack—it was just obvious that he hadn't felt the need to spruce himself up. It was, after all, just a trip to the grocery store.

His eyes swept over me as I shrugged on my coat. "You look nice."

"Thanks."

He sniffed the air. "Is that...Britney Spears?"

"Um, *no*," I scoffed. "You think I still wear that stuff?" I pushed past him into the hall, my cheeks burning. To be honest, I had a big bottle of it back home, too. Orion used to say I smelled like a twelve-year-old girl, but I didn't care. I had a million fond memories attached to that scent.

Kit shrugged. "Smells good, whatever it is. It brought back some memories for a second." He gave me a cautious half smile, and I wondered, with suddenly sweaty palms, exactly which ones he'd recalled.

"You know, it's nothing to be embarrassed about," he said after we'd gone silently down the stairs and settled into his car. He glanced into the rearview mirror and combed his fingers through his hair.

"What are you talking about?"

"Getting dressed up," he said. "You're single again, you probably don't get out much anymore...this is like a big night out for you. I get it."

"I get out plenty!" I said, slightly offended. "And look who's talking about having no life." I pulled a rolled-up copy of *Martha*

Stewart Living out of the center console and started reading one of the headlines in the voice of Mary Berry. "Transform your guest room into a five-star retreat!"

"Okay! Touché!" Kit laughed, grabbing the magazine out of my hand and tossing it into the backseat. "I was only kidding, anyway. I would have put in more effort myself if I'd had the time. But I came here straight from towing some knucklehead out of the river."

"Yikes. Almost puts Grandpa's little traipse through Dunkin' Donuts to shame. Was the knucklehead okay?"

"Arrested for DUI," said Kit, backing slowly out of the driveway. "But otherwise, doing just fine."

"You're a real American hero," I said. And then, after a pause, "So you'd have put in more effort if you'd had the time, huh?"

"That's the kind of man I am, Amy."

I looked thoughtfully out the window as we circled the common. *That's the kind of man I am.* All joking aside, what kind of man *was* he now? The person I'd left behind had been a teenaged boy. A good one, no doubt. But still, just a kid. I really had no clue what kind of a man he had turned out to be after all these years, and I suddenly found myself wanting very badly to find out.

"Tom didn't want to come?" asked Kit.

"No," I said, turning my attention away from the window. "We were at the store all afternoon, which was apparently enough excitement for him."

"How'd that go?"

"Not bad. I got to meet his millionaire stand-in-granddaughter, Josie, which was...enlightening."

Kit whistled. "The Powerball winner?"

"You know her?"

"She likes to bring coffee around to all the local businesses, it's sort of her thing. She's a character. A bit lonely, I think."

"Well, she's now a Pumpkin Everything employee. Or volunteer. I'm not sure exactly. Either way, she seems nice. And she'll be a big help in keeping the store open after I leave. That's what matters, right?"

"Of course," said Kit. He slowed down as we pulled onto Main Street. "I don't know about you, but I've got four flavors of Doritos at my house telling me grocery shopping on an empty stomach is a bad idea. Mind if we stop in The Plaid Apple for dinner first?"

"Sounds great."

"Do you remember when we came here after I got my driver's license?" asked Kit after we'd parked the car and were crossing the street.

"Of course," I said. "Your mother didn't want us driving too far, so we came here. I can still picture your mom, your grandmother, and both my parents all standing in the second-floor window. I'm pretty sure they watched us drive the entire way."

We paused our conversation while we stepped inside. I noticed that the door still stuck when you opened it, just as it always had, and smiled. The interior of the restaurant hadn't changed at all, either. Of course, with a name like The Plaid Apple, it was sort of hard to ever change your décor. Blue and red plaid valances with red appliquéd apples hung from the front windows, matching nicely with the red and blue fabric of the booths. All the walls were covered in oversized forks and spoons, rustic apple décor, and witty food-related signs. *Farm Fresh Apples 25 Cents. If You Don't Like My Standards of Cooking...Lower Your Standards.* The glass case beside the register was filled with apple muffins, pastries, and pies. A chalkboard on the wall listed the daily specials, including a turkey, cheddar, and Granny Smith sandwich, apple cinnamon pancakes, and caramel apple cider. This place was the apple lovers' answer to Pumpkin Everything.

We found ourselves a booth by the window and settled in. I spotted Moose Moriarty seated at the counter with Jackie Braeburn, the owner, standing behind it pouring him coffee. She was still wearing heavy black eyeliner, with her blonde bangs sprayed straight up, eighties style. I loved that she hadn't changed a bit.

"They weren't keeping an eye on us after dinner, though, were they?" asked Kit, drawing my attention back to our conversation. He gave me a wink and opened his menu.

After dinner? I wracked my brain, unable to think of what had happened after we'd left the diner that night. The silence went on for a beat too long, and Kit looked up at me.

"You don't remember," he said, looking at me over the top of his menu and furrowing his brow.

Staring for a moment into those green eyes, it hit me. "*Oh*," I said, shocked that he had brought it up, and equally shocked that I had forgotten. I sank down a few inches in the booth and let out a nervous chuckle. "Right. *That.*"

Okay, it's not what you're thinking. I mean, it's *almost* what you're thinking, but not quite. Kit and I never made it that far in our relationship. A few short weeks after that night, Rebecca was gone, and nothing between us was ever the same.

But that night...

We'd told our parents that we were going to see a movie after dinner. Instead, Kit had taken the two of us for a joyride down the Kancamagus scenic highway. Neither of our parents would have allowed it, being full of hairpin turns and suicidal moose just waiting for their chance to dart into oncoming traffic. But, like two giddy teenagers with a brand-new driver's license and a used Ford Focus, we'd hopped on the Kancamagus, pulled into a deserted scenic overlook, and made out for a good two hours.

It had been the first time we'd ever been truly alone like that. At the house, there was always the possibility of somebody walking in, so nothing much ever happened. But in that car, with only the looming, shadowy outline of Mt. Washington watching over us, things had quickly heated up. Shortly before deciding that we really did need to get home, we'd leaned back in our seats, gazing dopily into each other's eyes. *I love you,* he'd said, for the very first time. I said it back, without hesitation, as I'd already known it for years...and we didn't make it home for another hour and a half.

The sound of Moose hacking up a lung quickly pulled me back into the present. I fanned myself with a menu as I watched him slide off his stool and make his way outside, probably for a smoke. I tried thinking about disgusting things, like Garbage Pail Kids and kale, to bring my body temperature back down to normal, but nothing seemed to be working. Certainly not Kit Parker 3.0 looking at me from across the table with our shared, heated memories burning intently in his eyes.

Yeah. Totally not helpful.

CHAPTER 13

I buried my face in a menu, attempting to calm my hormones by reading all the options. There couldn't possibly be anything sexy about diner food. Caesar salad. French toast. Reuben. Extra-long hot dog.

Okay, not working.

Kit must've had the same plan because he cleared his throat and started reading all the items out loud. "Tuna melt, beef stew, meatball sub..." He flipped the menu over and studied the back. "Early bird specials start at four thirty. American Express accepted."

"I'm getting a cheeseburger," I announced, slamming my menu shut and shoving it back between the napkin holder and the condiments. "And apple pie for dessert. Of course."

"Of course," said Kit, joining his menu with mine. "Might as well make it two."

"Good evening," said Jackie, walking over with her notepad and two glasses of ice water. The words *Laconia Bike Week 2014* were stretched tightly across her chest. When she looked at me, her eyes lit up in recognition. "Amy Fox? I didn't know you were back in town! Must be because Tom went and plowed through that Dunks, huh?" She laughed loudly and glanced back at Moose who just shook his head.

"It could have happened to *anyone*," I said, defensively. As if Moose had any right to judgmentally shake his head—he'd driven between a moose's *legs,* for Pete's sake. "But yes, that's why I'm here. How have you been, Jackie?"

"Can't complain," she said, looking me over. "You write books now, don't you?"

Here we go. I gripped the edge of my seat and nodded politely. "Mmm hmm."

She tapped her pen against her notepad. "I've been meaning to read them, but things have just been too crazy around here with bike week and all."

I nodded my understanding. Bike week was in June. It was currently October. But, whatever.

"Don't worry about it," I said. "Most people haven't."

"No, no, no! Now that you're here, it'd be rude of me not to." She jotted my name down on her notepad and circled it about fifty times. "Now that that's settled, I don't know if I ever officially said congratulations to you, Kit. You just finished up that degree, right?"

"I did," said Kit, with a quick glance at me. "Resort Management. Thank you."

Resort Management? Kit had gone to college? That was news to me. The subject hadn't come up during any of our conversations. Of course, I'd been too afraid to ask for many details about his life after high school, and I suddenly felt very ashamed of myself.

"You think you can get the ball rolling now, on that be—" She was cut off by Kit's arm shooting out and knocking over his glass of water. Jackie jumped out of the way as it gushed over the edge of the table.

"Oh, geez," he said, grabbing a fistful of napkins. "I'm sorry. I don't know what happened there."

"No problem, hon." She gave him an odd look and a light bat to the back of the head, before hurrying away to grab some paper towels.

"So what's this about a Resort Management degree?" I asked once the mess had been cleaned up and we had placed our orders. "You didn't tell me you'd gone to college!"

Kit nodded. "After Riley finished, I figured it was time for me to give it a shot. Mom's life insurance left enough money for both of us to go if we wanted to."

"That's so great," I said, genuine tears coming to my eyes. "Your mom would be really proud. So...how come you're still driving the tow truck?"

Kit shrugged. "I only finished this past spring. I'm still planning my next move."

"Like, working at one of the ski resorts?"

"Something like that," he said vaguely. "Yeah."

It was unusual to have to pry information out of Kit, but I didn't press the issue. I just smiled at him across the table, truly happy to see him looking proud of himself. It was at that moment that I was struck by the idea that maybe he was planning to *leave* Autumnboro. My stomach sank. There were certainly resort jobs close by in the White Mountains, but there were also plenty of great jobs up in Maine or Vermont. Colorado. The Swiss Alps. Now that he'd gotten himself a degree, and Riley was all grown up, maybe he was feeling that it was finally time to leave and see the world. Not that it really made any difference to me. I would be going back to Pennsylvania in a few short weeks. Had I never come back, Kit could have taken a job in Kathmandu and it wouldn't have made a lick of difference. Only, I had come back. And my stomach was sinking.

We lapsed into an awkward silence after that, both of us resorting to fiddling around on our phones. I checked Facebook, only to find more comments about when my next book would be coming out. Great.

"So," Kit said, after placing his phone back down on the table. "Tell me. What's a day in the life of an accomplished author like? Back in Pennsylvania, I mean."

"Before or after accomplished author's big, sad breakup?" I asked, tossing my phone back into my bag.

"After," he said, studying my face. "If you woke up back there tomorrow, what would you do?"

I sighed. "Um, okay. I'd wake up in my half-empty bedroom because Orion took half the furniture with him when I threw him out. Then, I'd walk through my half-empty living room, where I'd see my wedding dress still hanging from the closet next to a big, sad pile of wasted wedding decorations."

"That's very Miss Havisham of you. What next?"

"Okay...after breakfast, I'd either sit on the couch with my laptop and stare at a blank Word document until lunchtime, or I'd go to Starbucks and stare at a blank Word document until lunchtime. Repeat until dinnertime. Netflix. Bed."

"Wow," said Kit. "That's pretty depressing. Even without the jilted bride component, which just takes it to a whole other level of gloom."

I flicked a sugar packet at him. "Thanks a lot."

"I wasn't trying to be mean," he said, catching the sugar packet and spinning it back at me. "It's cool that you have a routine. It just doesn't seem like a very healthy one."

"If I didn't stick to my routine, I wouldn't know what to do with myself." I shrugged. "I'd have to move my Netflix schedule up by, like, eight hours."

"Watching some quality Netflix might do you some good." He picked up our empty straw wrappers and started folding them into a paper spring. "Do you really think staring at a blank page all day is going to inspire you?"

"For your information, I've been inspired to open my own paper company. Reams of blank pages, as far as the eye can see!" I threw my arm out to the side. "And I won't be expected to write a single word on any of them. Dream come true."

Kit just raised his eyebrows.

"Okay, fine," I said. "Maybe you're right. But I have to keep showing up, even if I don't write anything. Isn't that how the quote goes? Ninety-nine percent of success is showing up?"

"True," said Kit pausing to take a sip of his soda. "Also true, the definition of insanity is doing the same thing over and over and expecting different results."

"That's actually not the definition of insanity. Why does everybody think that?"

"You know what I mean."

I frowned. "What *do* you mean?"

"I mean, no more staring at blank pages while you're here in Autumnboro. You're back for the first time in ten years, Amy. Just take it all in. Enjoy the store. Mingle with the townsfolk."

"I think I've already taken quite enough inspiration from the townsfolk."

He snorted. "I just mean, try to relax and be in the moment. You sound like you're putting too much pressure on yourself. It's usually when you stop trying so hard that the magic happens."

"The magic, huh? Isn't that what they tell people who are trying to get pregnant?"

"It's a broad concept, Ame." He tossed me the paper spring. "Give it a shot."

I nodded slowly, mulling over his words as I watched Moose return to his seat at the counter. Four high school kids came in behind him, tumbling goofily into a booth. I couldn't believe we were that young the last time we were here together.

"You've been missing out on so much since you've been gone," said Jackie, arriving at the table with our food. She placed it all down then leaned against the corner of the booth beside Kit. "Did you know that this one here's been volunteering with the Senior Citizens Council for almost ten years?"

"Really?" I asked, impressed. How many more secrets was he hiding from me? As he shrugged humbly, I caught a hint of pink forming on his cheeks.

"Sure. Every year he puts together a special event for the seniors. One year it was a fifties-style sock hop. Last year it was a masquerade ball. Not one of those regular costume parties with the skimpy kittens and the police officers with the skirts up to here." She slashed her hand across her upper thigh. "No, this was a classy black-tie, fancy dress sort of thing. All the old people wore those feathery, jeweled masks. My mother had the time of her life. So did Maggie and Tom!"

"Grandpa went to a masquerade ball?" I asked, looking from Jackie to Kit. "What's this year's theme?"

"I'm not sure yet," he said. "We're still kicking ideas around. We were thinking maybe an eighties biker bash. You'd be up for that, right Jackie?"

"Are you suggesting that I'm old enough for the senior center?"

"You'd be providing the food and drink. Obviously." He ducked out of the way as Jackie playfully swatted at the back of his head.

"*Obviously*." Jackie laughed then turned to me. "Despite the wise-guy routine, Kit here is one of the good ones. Isn't that right, Moose?" Moose held his coffee cup in the air in agreement, as did several other locals sitting around the counter.

That's the kind of man he is, I thought, happy that I hadn't needed to wait very long to find my answer. He was one of the good ones. Not that there'd ever been much doubt.

CHAPTER 14

"It's like a candy dispenser for pills," Mom explained into the phone the next morning. "It'll shout at him until he takes them."

She'd called to let me know that an installation technician for the Medi-Magic 3000—a state-of-the-art automatic pill dispenser—would be stopping by in an hour.

"That sounds terrible." I glanced into the living room where Grandpa was doing a crossword puzzle, classical music playing softly in the background. "Look, I went through his medications the other night and I think I've sorted it all out. I've set him up with one of those weekly organizers. He doesn't need some high-tech machine shouting at him."

"And who's going to refill that organizer once you're back home?"

I bit my lip, knowing full well how my answer would go over. "Grandpa?"

She laughed. "Tell me, Amy, what happens when he fills it incorrectly, ends up in the hospital, and I'm seven hours away?"

"Um..."

"That's what I thought," she continued. "The Medi-Magic

3000 gets excellent reviews. Isaac got one for his mother last year, and it's been a godsend. They provide a nurse to handle the refills, and for an extra five bucks a month, they'll text me his vitals. Although, what I'm supposed to *do* with his vitals, being seven hours away, I'm not quite sure."

"He's going to *love* that," I said, crinkling my nose as I poured myself some coffee. "Didn't I come up here so Grandpa wouldn't have to deal with a nurse?"

"So you're planning on staying there forever?"

I sighed. "No."

"I rest my case. How's everything else going? Was the store a disaster?"

"Not at all," I said, happy to inform her that Grandpa, with a little help, was still capable of running the store. I filled her in on new-hire Josie, my dinner with Kit, and some bits of town gossip. "I never realized how much I missed it here," I added. "It's kind of good to be back."

"Don't get too attached," she said. "Things can change in an instant. All it takes is one fall. One accidental overdose. One—"

"Okay, Mom. Geez. I get it." I caught Grandpa's eye and made a face as I pointed to the phone. "Look, I have to go, and you have a show to host in," I glanced at the clock, "ten minutes. Break a leg."

"That's not what they say for tele—"

I hung up before she could finish.

An hour later, Grandpa and I stood in the kitchen staring at the large white cylindrical machine taking up residence beside the toaster. It looked like a Dalek and a Keurig had made a baby.

"The Medi-Magic 3000 holds up to six doses per day," the technician explained after he had plopped the thing on the counter with more bravado than necessary. "It will announce *loudly and clearly*," he spoke the words both loudly and clearly, "when it's time for each dose to be taken." He pressed a few of the buttons on the base and took a step back.

"TIME FOR YOUR MEDICATION! PRESS BUTTON TO DISPENSE! TIME FOR YOUR MEDICATION! PRESS BUTTON TO DISPENSE!"

Grandpa and I jumped.

"It'll repeat the message every minute, for ninety minutes, until the patient has pressed the red button and retrieved the pill cup," said the technician, not at all fazed by the volume. He'd told us earlier that he'd been installing Medi-Magic 3000s for six years, so in all likelihood, he'd gone deaf.

"But can it stop me from flushin' 'em?" asked Grandpa, with a chuckle. I gave him a look.

"The machine will be loaded for the patient every week by one of our nurses," continued the technician as if Grandpa weren't even there. "I'll just do a quick demonstration." He filled several plastic cups with green Tic Tacs and pushed a button on the base of the machine. Like a secret laboratory in a sci-fi movie, a door slowly slid open revealing a hidden chamber. He placed the cups inside, shut the door, and pushed another button.

"TIME FOR YOUR MEDICATION! PRESS BUTTON TO DISPENSE!"

"Go on, try it," he said.

Grandpa reached out cautiously and pressed the red button. A cup full of green Tic Tacs slid out.

"Fantastic," he muttered.

"What happens if he's not home?" I asked, thinking of all the afternoons he spent at the senior center. "What if, say, after ninety minutes he still hasn't taken the dose?"

"If the patient misses a dose, the cup will slide into a special compartment, and the caregiver will be notified by an automated phone call."

An unsettling image of Mom receiving a call informing her that Grandpa had, for reasons unknown, missed a dose of his medication flashed through my head. When I talked to her earlier she seemed to be under the impression that this machine would eliminate all of her responsibilities. One robo-call from the Medi-Magic 3000 and she'd have him down in Pennsylvania within a week.

"Patient? Caregiver?" asked Grandpa. "What am I, an invalid?" Suddenly upset, he turned and walked out of the room. I followed after him into his bedroom, where I found him staring out the window and into the yard. The gauzy, pale blue curtains Gram had hung when I was young still covered the windows. The matching blue bedspread was piled on a chair where it had probably sat since she'd passed away.

"Hey," I said, gently putting my hand on his arm. "Mom ordered that silly thing to help you be able to stay here. To help you stay independent. So what if a nurse has to come by once a week to fill it?" I purposely left out the part about them checking his vitals and texting them off to Mom.

"It's going to be just like at the assisted living," he said. "Just like Maggie said. First, a nurse will come by to fill it. Then she'll ask for a spare key so she can get into the house without having to *trouble me*." He turned toward me and one-handedly air-quoted the words. "Next thing you know, she'll be loudly jiggling the doorknob to check if I'm dead."

"You're overreacting," I said, even though he wasn't. Not really.

"I was fine," said Grandpa, his voice catching on the last word. He walked over to the bureau and picked up a framed picture of him and Gram dressed in neon ski suits. "I was fine, until one stupid mistake. And now...now everybody's suddenly treating me like I'm *old*." He put down the photo and looked at me, my heart breaking at the sadness I saw in his eyes. "How did that *happen*, Amy?"

Whether he wanted to admit it or not, he *was* getting older. I felt a lump in my throat as I thought of all the time I'd been away, only seeing him on Christmas and Thanksgiving, never considering the fact that he wasn't always going to be around. I thought about the relationship we had missed out on having because I'd been so afraid of coming back here and facing up to Kit. On the other hand, the Grandpa I'd seen over the past few days didn't quite seem ready for any of this stuff.

"Look," I said. "You can either humor Mom by letting that machine yell at you a few times a day, or you can go back to your system of randomly taking your meds whenever you happen to remember and see how long it is before she moves you into an assisted living. Can we agree that neither one of us wants that?"

Grandpa looked at me curiously. "Why is it so important to you that I stay here? I'm trying not to take it personally that you prefer me being seven hours away."

"You know that's not why," I said, taking a seat on the bed. "I know how much you love it here. And, believe it or not, I love it here too. The thought of Mom selling this house, and me never being able to come back, it...well, it gives me chest pains. Every inch of this house reminds me of my happy childhood with you and Gram, and Mom and Dad, and—" I pointed toward the floor. For some reason I was very Lord Voldemort about speaking Kit's name in front of Grandpa. "This house is my last connection to him. And when I think about losing our last connection..." I trailed off and shook my head. "Chest pains."

"We're in the same boat then," said Grandpa. He picked up the framed photograph again and carried it over to the bed, sitting down beside me. "This is where we lived for our entire marriage. Where we raised our children. Where we spent every holiday. This house is my last connection to her, too. I won't say it gives me chest pains to think about losing it, though, or you might hit the panic button on that machine out there."

I laughed and wiped away a tear that had escaped. "You know, I do have one other reason for not wanting Mom to sell."

"What's that?"

"Whatever would we tell Walter?"

Grandpa chuckled. When I was a kid, hanging out in the

Parkers' apartment downstairs, I'd sometimes hear footsteps from above even when I knew that my family wasn't home. Instead of telling me it was my imagination, or the house settling, Grandpa had written out a list of all the people who had once lived here. We'd decided together that we were being haunted by Walter Roundbottom, Esquire, the unsmiling solicitor who had lived here from 1864 to 1887. Grandpa told me that he was haunting us as payback for everybody always giggling about his name. I didn't sleep for a week, but I appreciated the creativity. And the honesty. Perhaps it was a bit of both.

"Come on," I said, standing up and heading for the door. "We'll let that knucklehead finish his spiel, then we can make fun of Mom on TV until the senior van gets here. I know that always cheers *me* up."

"A girl after my own heart," said Grandpa, following me out of the room. "Fantastic."

CHAPTER 15

After Grandpa had been picked up by the senior center shuttle, I walked by myself to Pumpkin Everything. Grandpa felt bad about sending me off to the store alone, but Barbara Cortland was bringing in her Blu-Ray copy of *Jurassic World*, and he hadn't wanted to miss it. I didn't mind. Josie was coming in for the afternoon, but even if she weren't, the idea of having some alone time at the store seemed sort of nice.

As I straightened up the merchandise and chatted with customers, I felt a strong connection to my grandmother that I'd never really experienced before. I felt as if I were seeing, through her eyes, what it must have been like working day after day in the business she had built up out of hard work and love. I met some lovely families from Oklahoma and Oregon and a sweet elderly couple who'd come all the way from California. Everybody was thrilled to be in New Hampshire at the height of fall foliage season, and pumpkin everything was flying off the shelves. It was warm and enjoyable, and being immersed in so many fall scents was even starting to become easier. How could a bag of potpourri make me want to puke when that sweet old woman from California said it reminded her of her grandma? Impossible!

When things slowed down, I sat behind the counter with my laptop open and started jotting down some ideas. It was more note-taking than novel writing, but I was more optimistic than I'd been in months, and I wanted to take advantage of the feeling. It wasn't until Josie walked in that I realized I'd completely forgotten about lunch.

"You're lucky you hired me," she said, holding two paper bags in the air. "I stopped at Autumnboro Pizza just in case you guys hadn't eaten yet."

"You don't have to keep doing that," I said, inhaling the delicious smell of garlic coming from the bags. "Although, I'm glad you did. Thank you."

"My pleasure," she said, pulling way too many paper-wrapped sandwiches out of the bag and placing them on the counter. "I brought two meatball parms, a chicken parm, an eggplant parm, and a cold veggie, just in case you were into that sort of thing. Where's Tom?"

"Senior center." My stomach rumbled as I grabbed one of the meatball subs.

"Ah. Maybe I'll swing the rest of these by the funeral home. Although, those guys could stand to get out for lunch once in a while." She shuddered.

"You know, it's really nice that you bring food and coffee to everybody in town," I said. "That's like...above and beyond."

She shrugged as she unwrapped her sandwich. "It's no biggie."

"I like your top, by the way," I said, tipping my chin toward her pink and white-striped tunic. "Isaac Mizrahi?"

"Who else? Your mom said they had very limited quantities, so I ordered six while I still could."

"*Six?*"

"One in each color."

"I'll let you in on a little secret," I said, pulling a stack of napkins out from beneath the counter. "My mom likes to say that things have limited quantities when in reality, they have more than they know what to do with. Most of my Christmas presents consist of QVC overstock. Excuse me a minute." I walked across the store to help a customer trying to reach a precariously balanced wooden sign.

"So, how long are you actually going to be here for?" Josie asked, after I'd come back.

"A few weeks?" I said, sinking onto a stool. "I came up to check on my grandfather and to make sure that the store was in good shape. Once his wrist is better," I shrugged, "I guess that's it."

"Have you considered staying, though? It'd be kind of nice having someone my own age around here. Everyone in town is really nice, don't get me wrong...it's just that we don't really have a lot in common. I mean...Moose? Jackie? They're all *blah blah blah, this thing happened thirty years ago, blah blah blah, my back hurts.* Besides, it's not like you have any..."

She trailed off, shaking her head and taking a big bite of her sandwich. *It's not like you have anybody back in Pennsylvania,* was what she had almost said. That's what she and Grandpa must chat about over coffee. Me. He hadn't told Kit, or Susan, or his friends at the senior center about my love life, but he'd apparently confided in the nice girl who looked a lot like me. Not that I could blame him.

"What do I know about running a country store?" I asked, letting the awkward moment pass.

She shrugged. "About as much as Tom did when the store was left to him."

"But the store belonged to his *wife*," I pointed out. "Taking over the store from her was, like...required. I'm just the granddaughter. I have my own life down in Pennsylvania. I have a condo, and my parents, and a full-time writing career..." I ticked each item off on my fingers, well aware that I hadn't even filled an entire hand.

"You're not *just* the granddaughter," she said. "You're *the* granddaughter. Tom's told me all about your uncle Pete and how he has five boys. Never mind that they all live in Utah. Have you thought about what's going to happen to the store after Tom, you know...*moves on?*"

When did this conversation turn so depressing? I stared at my paper plate, morosely chewing on a meatball, unsure of how to answer.

"I'm sorry," added Josie, quickly. "I wasn't trying to guilt you into anything. I just...I really like this place. I'd hate to see it turned into an H&R Block or something." She slid off her stool and walked toward the back room. "Speaking of your writing career, I've been meaning to read one of your books. I'm going to grab one right now. I saw a few on a shelf out back."

"You really don't have to," I called after her.

But she was already gone, returning a minute later with a pristine copy of *Nightlife Negative*. "Where do you get your ideas from?" she asked, scanning the back cover.

"Um, here and there." I cleared my throat. "It's hard to know exactly."

"You working on anything new?"

"Not yet. I'm sort of waiting for inspiration to strike." I thought about what Kit had said the other night—about living in the moment and not putting so much pressure on myself. Taking over the store would certainly be a step in that direction. Although, it could also be seen as a step in the direction of completely giving up. And living here in Autumnboro again, after all this time? In the same house as Kit? That would be beyond bizarre.

"If inspiration's what you're looking for, you've come to the right place. This town is full of characters."

I snorted. "You have no idea."

After Josie had taken off to deliver the rest of the food to the funeral home, I decided it was past time to make a call to Donnie at the auto shop. The phone rang about fourteen times before he answered.

"Probably gonna need to order some parts," he said.

"Um, okay. When will you know for sure?"

"Few days," he said.

"And...how long before they come in?"

"Few more."

"Right," I said, blowing out a breath. "Okay, well, you've got my number. Thanks, Donnie."

"At least you're not dealing with that Ronnie character," he practically shouted into the phone before I could hang up. "That guy's a *real* idiot. You'd probably never get your car back if you were dealing with *him*."

I closed my eyes. "You've been reading my books, have you?"

"Oh yeah, downloaded one the other day. Almost done with it. Anyway, like I said, it'll be a while." He slammed down the phone before I could say anything else.

Fantastic.

* * *

GRANDPA JOINED us at the store for the rest of the week—showing both me and Josie the ropes—and appearing to be in higher spirits than I'd seen since his accident. We'd just arrived back home on Friday evening, when Kit popped out of his apartment. We'd barely seen each other since the night we'd gone to dinner and grocery shopping. Speaking of which, the way he was dressed reminded me of how overdressed I'd been that night. Almost as if I thought we were going on a—

Ah, crap.

"Hey," he said, smiling at me as he locked his door. "Long time, no see. Again."

"I'll give you two a minute," said Grandpa, heading up the stairs.

"Be careful," I called after him, cringing as he lifted his good hand off the railing to bat it dismissively at me. I waited until he was safely inside before turning my attention back to Kit.

"Not quite as long this time," I said, trying to act casual. Trying not to stare at his crisp, button-up shirt and dark, non-tow-truck-driver-looking jeans. "Got a hot date or something?"

Of course, he had a hot date. This was exactly the reason why I couldn't move back here and take over the store. The only thing more awkward than seeing Kit all the time would be seeing Kit going out on hot dates all the time. Sure, I had almost married somebody else. But I hadn't expected Kit to watch me walk down the aisle.

He ran his hand through his hair, suddenly looking uncomfortable. "I made plans a few weeks ago," he said. "I had no idea that you would be—"

"No, it's cool," I cut in. "Even if you'd known I would be here...why would that have mattered?"

"It...it wouldn't have," he said, jingling his keys around in his hand. "I just meant...we're cool?"

"Super cool."

That's me. Super cool. I turned and walked stiffly up a few steps, wishing one of them would drop out from under me, sending me down into the bowels of the Earth. "Have fun. I'll see you later."

"Tomorrow?"

"Huh?" I stopped halfway up the stairs and turned around.

"Do you want to, maybe, do some sightseeing tomorrow? This will be your first weekend back. I thought you might like to see some of the old spots again."

Looking down at him, I noticed that his pale green eyes were lost in the light gray plaid of his shirt. I felt a swell of relief that whomever he was going on a date with wouldn't be getting their full impact. Not that he didn't look good. But put him in a darker color—forest green, navy blue, black—and she'd be a goner.

Whoever she was. For some reason, I didn't want to ponder it further. I walked slowly back down a few steps until we were at eye level.

"You want to take me sightseeing tomorrow, after your hot date tonight?"

"I thought you said we were cool?"

We stared at each other for a few seconds. An unspoken challenge hung heavily in the air.

"I'll meet you outside, bright and early," I said. "Eight o'clock."

I smiled to myself as I turned and ran up the stairs. Might as well make it difficult for his hot date to spend the night.

CHAPTER 16

It was cold the next morning when I stepped onto the front porch. But it was warm inside my hiking jacket and hat, and I took a moment to breathe in the crisp, clean air as a curtain of leaves rained down in front of me. Everywhere I looked—from the church across the common to the woman in a University of New Hampshire sweatshirt walking her dog—was so quintessentially New England that my heart squeezed with affection for my home state.

I was excited to do some sightseeing today, and not only because it would involve spending time with Kit. It had been years since I'd experienced the natural beauty that had once been a part of my everyday life. Years since I stood ankle deep in the ice-cold water of the Pemigewasset River, breathing in nature, humbly aware that I was the only person on the planet currently standing in that particular spot. Over the years, I hadn't really allowed myself to think about what I had given up when I'd left this place.

But now, the side of me that used to enjoy communing with nature and having philosophical thoughts out in the woods seemed to be waking up. I took a deep breath as I pressed my palms against the porch railing, closing my eyes as I let it out. *Of all the people on the planet, I'm the only one standing in this spot, at this moment.* I never talked about that sort of thing with Orion. I'd learned very quickly that he viewed it all as tree-hugging mumbo jumbo. But I stood there now, alone, letting all my hippy-dippy thoughts and feelings wash over me.

A moment later, the front door creaked open.

"Beautiful, huh?" asked Kit, joining me at the railing. "I love to sit out here in the morning while I drink my coffee. I like to think about how nobody else has this exact view at this exact moment."

I nodded and cast him an amused, sidelong glance. His outfit was almost an exact replica of mine—black North Face jacket with a wool hat. He rested his hand on the railing next to mine, his left pinky casually brushing up against my right.

"So, my hot date ended pretty early," he added, staring out at the lawn. A squirrel darted down one of the oak trees and ran around in a frantic circle.

"Oh?" I sensed him turning to look at me but kept my eyes glued to the squirrel who faked right, faked left, then darted back up the tree.

"Yeah. It was a Tinder thing. I definitely should've swiped left."

"Too bad," I said, forcing a chuckle. I felt nauseated at the thought of him swiping at pictures of women on Tinder. Swiping right, swiping left...what did it all even mean? Having never needed to use a dating app myself, I was a total old fogey about them. I pictured nothing but sexting and invitations to anonymous, kinky orgies.

As I stood there pondering the meaning of Tinder, I felt Kit's pinky move a fraction of an inch closer to mine. Rather than pulling away, I allowed myself to sink into it. And while a pinky finger sinking into another pinky finger is probably the lamest thing imaginable to anyone on Tinder, it was actually pretty amazing. From that minuscule point of contact, came a huge spark of electricity. We stood there for a few seconds—my heart suddenly pounding, my body afraid to move lest it break our minuscule point of contact—both of us silently staring out across the common. The woman I'd seen walking her dog glanced up at us, probably wondering why we were standing there frozen like a couple of weirdos. I swallowed.

"Let's blow this popsicle stand," I said, sliding my hand over his and pulling him gently away from the railing. He squeezed my hand and followed me down the porch steps to his car.

It was only a ten-minute drive up Route 3 to get to the Flume. With its ninety-foot granite walls, rushing waterfalls, and boardwalks, the Flume was the ultimate nature walk, and one of my favorite places to visit as a kid. When I saw the sign for it on the side of the highway—dark wood with carved, yellow bubble letters—I let out an audible squeal of glee.

Kit glanced over and smiled.

"How often do you come here?" I asked after we had purchased our tickets and were making our way up the dirt path into the woods.

"Not very," he said. "I usually save the Flume for when I have tourists in town." He lightly punched me in the arm.

"I am *not* a tourist," I said, a bit stung by the word. I may just be visiting, but this was still the place where I had grown up. My family still owned a house here, for Pete's sake. Just because I hadn't been back in a long time didn't make me a tourist. It wasn't like I had a guidebook, and a camera, and—

I quickly slid my tourism pamphlet and my phone back into my purse. Kit snorted and flicked at the sticker on my jacket. *I Hiked The Flume Gorge, New Hampshire.*

"They gave it to me with my ticket," I said, rolling my eyes. "What was I supposed to do? Throw it away?"

Kit just shook his head.

"What?"

"It's funny."

"What's funny?"

"That you're so excited to be here," he said. "After, you know...you couldn't get out of here fast enough."

I kept walking, trying to ignore his comment. I kicked a few pebbles at him with the side of my foot. He kicked a few back at me. By the time we stopped at Table Rock—a section of the Flume where the water rushes over a wide granite slab, which Kit, Riley, and I always thought would make a fantastic waterslide—his comment had gotten fully underneath my skin.

"You know," I said, staring out at the rushing water. "It's not fair to tell me that I couldn't get out of here fast enough." I turned to face him. "I mean, I know I was awful for leaving, but I had my reasons. Even if they were selfish, and even if I regretted them later on, they seemed right when I was seventeen. So, don't imply that I just left on some...some flaky whim." I made *flaky whim* motions with my hands.

"I know you didn't leave on a whim," he said, his brow furrowing. "Of course I know that. Why are you being so hard on yourself?"

I looked at him, wide-eyed with disbelief. "Because I broke up with you for not wanting to take me to the *prom*."

"Yeah, but that wasn't the real reason," he said, coming closer until we were only a few feet apart. "That was just the last straw."

"But it was such a small thing," I said, a lump forming in my throat. Were we really going to have this conversation now? In public? I glanced toward the dirt path, but there didn't seem to be anyone else around this early. So I supposed we were.

"Straw's a small thing, Amy," he said. "It's flimsy. That's the whole point of saying that something was *the last straw*. I know I wasn't an easy person to be with senior year, and you did nothing but try to help me." He reached out and gently stroked the side of my hair.

"But I could have tried harder," I said, fighting back tears as I spoke my biggest regret in life out loud. "I just...I gave up. I *left* you. Whatever reasons I thought I had, they didn't hold up after I'd gone."

"Hey," he said, stepping closer and wrapping his arms around me. "It was never on you to fix me. You know that, right?"

I buried my head in his chest and shook my head.

"I needed more than you could have ever given me," he said, pulling back just enough to look at me. "And that wasn't your fault. What I needed back then was beyond either of us, okay?"

When I responded with a feeble shrug, he led me over to a large rock by the edge of the water, and we sat down side by side. He put his arm around me and I leaned my head against his shoulder, which was about a million times nicer than brushing pinkies. How was he being so forgiving?

"Let me tell you my story," he said, once we were settled. "After you'd gone off to college, I spent another entire year in a fog, just plodding through life. Angry and lost. I wasn't in school anymore, so I got a job over at Moose's. But, he had to let me go after a few weeks because I didn't always show up. Then Donnie gave me a job at his place, detailing cars, but the same thing happened. My grandmother tried to get me into counseling, but I didn't want to hear it." He paused, turning his head toward me. "You know how stubborn I could be."

With my head still on his shoulder, I nodded.

"Eventually," he continued, "it was Riley who convinced me to go to therapy. He told me that if I was going to give up college in order to be around for him, then maybe I should try to be more like someone he actually wanted to be around."

"Ouch."

"Yeah. He's got a way with words. But it did the trick. It convinced me to go and talk to a therapist who got me on some medication, which lifted the clouds enough for me to start moving forward. My first assignment was to find myself a hobby that I thought I might enjoy. I couldn't think of a single thing, so I signed up for a quilting class at the senior center."

"A quilting class?" I lifted my head and looked at him skeptically.

He smiled. "Yep. Usually you need to be sixty-five, but everyone in town knew my mom and felt sorry for me, so they let me join. I didn't talk to anybody at first. My plan was to skate by under the radar and just get this ridiculous *find a hobby* part of my therapy over with. There was a part of me that wanted to prove that having a hobby wasn't going to magically get me over the death of my mother. I was angry that my therapist, who hadn't been through what I'd been through, could think she had all the answers. You know?"

I nodded, and my heart broke as I pictured Kit at seventeen again, his pain and grief still so fresh and all-consuming.

"Anyway, the other people in the class, they wouldn't let me skate by under the radar. They kept trying to pull me into their conversations about grandchildren and arthritis. Things I had zero interest in. But eventually, they started talking about other parts of their lives, and it turned out that most of them knew *exactly* what I was going through. These were people in their seventies and eighties, and they'd all lost parents. Not as young as I had, but that didn't matter. I started feeling more comfortable around them, opening up more, and fifty-year age gap or not, it was another big step in the right direction. That's why I volunteer with the Senior Citizens Council. To try to pay them back for everything they did for me."

When he finished speaking, he looked at me for a reaction.

I smiled.

"I'm still sorry that I wasn't there for you," I said, taking his hand and squeezing it. "But I'm so glad that you found some people who were."

As I felt the warmth of his hand in mine, a huge weight lifted from my chest. He had found what he'd needed, in his own way, in his own time, and the clouds that plagued him had lifted. It hadn't been thanks to me, but that was okay. *He* was okay. And that was the only thing that mattered.

CHAPTER 17

At the sound of voices coming up the path, we reluctantly climbed down from our rock and continued on our hike into the Flume Gorge. The air cooled significantly as we made our way higher and higher, up the wooden ramps and steps between the towering granite walls. Water roared beneath us, cascading down over the rocks, and filling the air with mist. At one time, a huge boulder had hung suspended between the narrow granite walls. It had fallen in 1883, and nobody knows for sure where it ended up. Kit, Riley, and I would always try to find it, pointing at boulder after boulder, asking Grandpa to take pictures of us standing on top of each one, just in case. It wasn't quite Space Mountain, but we had fun.

When we reached the top of the boardwalk, we came out onto the hiking trail that would take us back to the Visitor Center. After a few minutes of walking, I darted off the path and picked a thick stick up off the ground.

"Walking stick!" I announced, proudly heaving it forward with every step and planting it into the ground like Gandalf. As kids, we had always competed for who could find the biggest walking stick, a game that was possibly even more boring than searching for a long-lost boulder. But like I said, we had fun.

"You call that a walking stick?" asked Kit. He jogged ahead and veered off into the woods. When he returned to the path, he was dragging a small tree. I burst out laughing.

"A *stick,* Kit. The game is to find a *stick!*"

"I don't know what you're talking about," he said, swinging it forward with all his strength. He planted it in the ground, sending up a huge puff of dirt. He started swinging it forward again just as a massive crack of thunder sounded from above. I screamed, and Kit dropped the branch to the ground as the downpour started.

We were both drenched by the time we made it to a rain shelter further along the path. We sat huddled together, laughing and cold, on the bench against the back wall, looking out into the rain.

Another crack of thunder had me covering my ears. Thunderstorms were so much more intense out here in the woods. Kit put an arm around my shoulders, which, despite his intentions, did absolutely nothing to calm my nerves. All it did was remind me of that time in the gondola at Loon. I turned my head to look up at him, meeting his eyes, and then—

"Oy, we made it!" A loud, abrasive voice cut in, ruining the moment and making me jump. "Richard, get in here!"

I looked up to find an older woman, dressed in a pale blue rain slicker and jeans that swung above her ankles, shaking out an umbrella. She beckoned, with exaggerated arm motions, to somebody still outside. A moment later, a man appeared behind her, his wispy gray hair sticking out in every direction. I fought back a giggle at the thought that perhaps he'd already been struck by lightning—which, I know, is *not* funny in the slightest. But he was wearing both a fanny pack and a backpack and looked disoriented—as if he'd been peacefully reading the newspaper on the toilet, when he found himself inexplicably beamed into the forest. I bit my tongue.

"Room for two more?" asked the woman.

"Of course," said Kit, sliding a few inches away from me. "You don't want to be stuck out there in this."

"A thunderstorm in October! How were we to know?" The woman made dramatic *how were we to know* motions with her hands before ordering Richard to pull water and snacks from the backpack. "I'm Joan, by the way. Joan Hartwell. This is my husband, Richard."

Richard saluted us before fishing the requested items from the backpack and producing a couple of ShamWows from the fanny pack. He offered them to Kit and me before pulling out two more and going to work on drying off his wife.

"How long have you two been married?" asked Kit, which was the obvious question to ask when a couple starts towel-drying each other in public.

I glanced at him, smiling.

"Forty-two years," said Joan, rolling her eyes. "We've been coming up here from Massachusetts every summer and fall. This one's been coming here since he was a kid." She motioned roughly to Richard. "He's a real nut about it."

"So is my grandpa," I said, my heart melting for Richard. "He's lived here his whole life and he's still a nut about it. He even built this beautiful model Concord coach. When I was a kid, he got special permission to climb inside the one in the Visitor Center so he could take pictures."

Richard's eyes bugged out of his head. "They let him *inside*?"

"Oy, please," said Joan. "Don't give him any ideas. Our house is already filled with enough old crap."

"So is my grandpa's," I said fondly. "You guys should meet."

Joan gave me a disapproving look, and I quickly busied myself with checking the radar on my phone. It looked like we might be stuck in the rain shelter for a while. While Kit chatted with

Richard and Joan about the Red Sox, and whether or not the long-lost Flume boulder actually existed, I pondered the idea of being married to somebody for forty-two years. I did the calculations. If I were to get married tomorrow, that would make me seventy years old. I let out a small sigh of relief that I wasn't going to be spending all those years trapped in a marriage with Orion Corcoran. Sitting there next to Kit, our issues finally resolved, I could barely remember how that had ever seemed like a good idea.

"I think we might be good to go," I said half an hour later as I checked the radar one last time. The storm had passed and the sky was blue again, though it was sort of a shame we wouldn't get any alone time in the shelter after all. We said goodbye to Richard and Joan and hiked our way back to the Visitor Center.

From the Flume, we drove to Clark's Trading Post, which was open for its final weekend of the season. We had lunch, watched the trained bear show, and took the classic train ride through the woods where we were chased by the iconic "Wolfman" in his rickety old jalopy. It had been much too long since I screamed, "Scram, you old goat!" at the grizzly actor, who was probably just somebody's sweet old grandpa. He used to terrify me as a child, and even now, as I sat laughing with Kit, I felt an irrational flicker of fear that he would somehow catch up to us and board the train. Which, of course he never did. A familiar feeling of relief washed over me once the train had crossed the covered bridge, marking the end of Wolfman territory. At that point, I supposed he drove back into the woods to have a smoke and check Facebook, before tormenting the next group of tourists. Which is apparently what I was today. A *tourist*. Although, the word didn't bother me as much as it had that morning. I accepted the fact that I'd lost some of that familiarity and boredom that comes with being a local and was indeed seeing everything with fresh, touristy eyes. And it was *fun.* I smiled as I flipped through the free guidebook that I'd picked up at the ticket counter, wondering when we could squeeze in a visit to the Polar Caves.

"One more stop?" Kit asked as we got back into the car.

"Yes, please," I said, happy to keep the day going for as long as possible. "Where to?"

The sun was getting low in the sky, and the temperature was dropping as we walked down the long path to Profile Lake. We sat on the stone wall at the edge of the beach and looked up at Cannon Mountain where the Old Man of the Mountain used to be—the famous granite profile of a human face that crumbled to the ground in 2003.

"I always think about when that first park ranger noticed he was gone," I said. "After the fog cleared, she looked up, and it just wasn't there anymore." I shook my head. It was sort of lame, but that hunk of granite always got to me.

"I know the feeling," said Kit, gently nudging me with his knee.

I slid off the wall and walked over to one of the coin-operated binoculars. I stood on the top rung and looked through the viewer into blackness. I didn't have any quarters on me. Not that there was anything to look at anymore, anyway. And even if there were, I could just zoom in on it with my phone. They'd probably haul those old coin-operated monstrosities away eventually—a thought that was sort of sad. I took a picture of the faceless mountain, which was also sort of sad, and put my phone back into my purse.

Kit came over to join me then, his hands jammed into his pockets. We were all alone on the edge of the lake, it being either too late or too cold for the tourists. The fact that I was there proved that I wasn't *truly* one of them. Sure, I was enough of a tourist to appreciate all the things I'd once taken for granted. But unlike a tourist, for me, there wasn't any other place that felt more like home. Pennsylvania, at the moment, seemed a million miles away.

I took a step closer to Kit and pulled his left hand gently out of his pocket, holding it in mine. I had tried to start a new life, in a new state, with a new man...and somehow, all of it had led me straight back here. I gently pulled his right hand out of his other pocket.

He looked down at me intently, for only a moment, before sliding both hands around my waist and leaning in to kiss me. His lips were so warm and familiar, that my hands were around his neck in an instant, afraid I might lose him again if I didn't hold on tight. I kissed him back, twisting my fingers into his hair and pulling him close, wanting to make sure he knew how much I had missed him. After a while, we made our way back to the car, where we stayed until long after the sun had gone down. We stayed until there was no longer any doubt that he knew exactly how I felt.

* * *

As we walked up the porch steps to the house, Kit pulled me to the side before I could unlock the front door.

"Close your eyes for a second."

I obeyed, hoping that maybe he was going to kiss me some more. "I want you to think about today. You, and me, and everything that happened."

"Okay."

"Whatever you do, don't open your eyes." A moment later, the scent of the pumpkin spice candle was thrust beneath my nose. I made a face and took a step back.

"Whoa, whoa, whoa," said Kit, grabbing my arm before I backed right down the steps. "Take it easy. Just breathe it in and think about today."

I swallowed, relaxed my face, and did what he asked. Memories of months of wasted wedding planning, broken hearts, and lost deposits crashed up against pleasant memories of this dreamlike day. I breathed in deeply and opened my eyes.

"Better?"

"Better."

He put the candle back down on the table, took me into his arms, and kissed me some more.

Oh, yes, definitely better.

CHAPTER 18

The following morning, I was on a bus full of senior citizens, headed to the factory outlets down in Tilton for a day of shopping with Grandpa. Senior center bus trips weren't my typical idea of a good time, but Kit was scheduled to work, and I needed something to keep my mind occupied. Despite a pleasant end to the previous evening, I'd had a restless night full of uneasy dreams. In them, Kit kept telling me that he was leaving not just Autumnboro, but the entire country. He was moving to Australia...to Thailand...to Cabo San Lucas. *I'm opening a bed-and-breakfast in the South China Sea.* Clearly, my subconscious was afraid that whatever we had started wasn't going to last. And my subconscious probably had a good point.

I closed my eyes and tried to focus, instead, on the positive. They flew open again almost immediately. Focusing on the positive aspects of last night was a bit awkward while sitting there beside my grandfather. Changing gears, I slipped on my headphones and was about to listen to an audiobook, when a voice came from across the aisle.

"We always wondered if we'd ever get to meet you," it said, as something poked me sharply in the arm. I jerked my arm away and took out my headphones. There was a woman seated across from me with short, curly white hair and long pink fingernails, one of which had jabbed me in the bicep. "Tom's told us a lot about you."

"What does Tom know about her?" cut in a man sitting one row back. "Tom, do you know this woman?"

"She's his granddaughter!" shouted another white head, swiveling around a few rows up. "He introduced us the other day! You were all there!"

"Whose granddaughter?"

"Tom's!"

Now all sorts of elderly heads and necks were craning over and around seats, trying to get a look at Grandpa who simply rolled his eyes.

"Who do you think I'm sitting with? My new girlfriend?" he asked. "She's my granddaughter! The one who writes the scary books!"

"We know!" said the first man. "You tell us about her every day!"

"Well, you just asked!"

He batted a hand at Grandpa and slumped down into his seat.

"As I was *saying*," said the first woman, pausing to sigh, "it's lovely to finally meet you. I'm Evelyn, and I've always loved a good, scary story. Especially Edgar Allen Poe."

"That raven," said the man behind her, pointing a finger in the air. "He was something."

"And that's Walter," said Evelyn, tipping her head. "Don't mind him."

"It's nice to meet both of you," I said, nodding to Walter who still seemed lost in thought about "The Raven." "But, I wouldn't exactly compare myself to Edgar Allen Poe."

"Nonsense," said Evelyn, producing a phone from her handbag and clacking at the screen with her pink nails. "I've been meaning to read your books. I really have. It's just that every time I try to read *anything*, I fall right to sleep."

I nodded along sympathetically. Falling asleep as soon as their eyes hit the page was a common affliction among the non-readers of the world. Or so I'd learned over the years.

"It's fine," I said. "Really. Don't bother."

"No, no!" She stretched her phone out in front of her and peered at the screen through her bifocals. "I'm going to make a point of staying awake to read one of *yours*. Which one do you suggest?"

"*Bad Reception* is on sale for two ninety-nine!" cut in a woman from the back of the bus. "Downloading it now!"

I stood up in my seat and turned around to see who was speaking, and—oh, no. As soon as I did, my stomach sank. It was Barbara Cortland—purveyor of *Jurassic World* Blu-Rays and long-time substitute teacher in the Autumnboro school district. Her jet-black dye job and fuchsia lipstick had followed me all the way from kindergarten through twelfth grade and then straight into the pages of my books. Her fictitious counterpart was the principal of Fallsburg High School—a total stickler who ran the school like a military prison yet managed to allow the senior prom to get overthrown by satanic cult members. Fantastic.

"Mrs. Cortland?" I said weakly, still hanging onto hope that it was merely her doppelganger. Some sort of Lynchian, Black Lodge-type phenomenon would be amazing right now.

"That's right," she said in her familiar, no-nonsense way of speaking. All hope of doppelgangers fell to the wayside. "I'll start on that book right away." She flipped her phone around, showing me the Amazon screen where she had just one-click-ordered my worst nightmare.

"Me too," said Evelyn, proudly showing me her screen, as well.

"Me too!" chimed in another voice, and then another, and another. I looked around in horror. Nearly the entire bus full of old people were holding up their cell phones like teenagers at a rock concert, all showing receipts for the purchase of my books.

"Thank you," I managed. "That's....that's very kind. I'll just…I'll be going now." I sank slowly back down into my seat and pinched the bridge of my nose.

"You all right?" asked Grandpa.

I removed my hand and peered sardonically up at him. "You've read my books, haven't you?"

"Sure." He shrugged.

"And?"

"You may have taken a few liberties. But it's not like you wrote anything that wasn't true."

"And you think that's going to *help*?"

"Here," he said, rifling inside his jacket pocket. "Have a root beer stick."

I rolled my eyes, but I took the candy. And I had to admit, it did make me feel a bit better.

* * *

"I WAS WONDERING if it would be all right if I had a guest over for dinner tonight?" Grandpa asked, as he dug into his eggs the next morning.

"You know you don't have to ask my permission to have a guest over," I said. "This is your house. Let me guess, Maggie?"

"Well, yes. But don't worry, you aren't going to need to cook for us or anything."

"I wouldn't mind," I said, taking a sip of coffee. "I was thinking of making spaghetti tonight. That's easy enough to double."

"No, no. We usually order Chinese takeout once a week and watch old movies."

"That's so sweet," I said, picturing Grandpa and Maggie holding hands on the couch, wondering if it would be weird to sneak a picture to send Mom. "Go right ahead. I won't disrupt your routine."

"There is a bit more to it," he said, laying down his fork.

I raised my eyebrows. "It's just that...sometimes...she...*stays over*." He said the words slowly and deliberately and I choked on my coffee.

"Oh," I said after I'd finished coughing. "Okay. I gotcha." Right. So, hand-holding on the couch isn't all that's on their agenda for the night. I will *not* be taking pictures to send Mom after all. Ew. Okay, *breathe* Amy. They're both adults. It's cool. I mean, I just hadn't taken this sort of thing into account. Although, that expired bottle of Viagra I'd found was starting to make a lot more sense.

"It's just that Maggie lives over at Winter's Eve," he continued, "and the nurses are always popping in with the master key to check if she's dead..."

"Nope, nope, I get it!" I practically shouted. "No need to explain." I stood and started rapidly clearing away plates. "You know what? I never returned Kit's spare key!" I threw the plates into the sink, grabbed the key that had been sitting on the kitchen counter for the past few days, and hightailed it out of the apartment. I shuddered as I closed the door behind me.

Grandpa and Maggie. Cool. Whatever.

I shuddered again at the bottom of the stairs. Sorry, no. Not cool. Not whatever. I mean, it's *Grandpa*.

I knocked loudly on the door to the Parkers' apartment. No response. They'd probably both already left for work. I fingered the spare key in my hand, feeling a bit weird about just letting myself in. But I didn't want to go back upstairs just yet. Technically, I was Kit's landlord. It wasn't like I needed a warrant to go inside. And I wasn't planning to snoop around or anything. All I wanted to do was put the key back in the kitchen drawer and avoid talking to my grandfather about his sex life. Who could fault me for that? I slipped the key into the lock and stepped inside, going straight to the kitchen and putting the key back in the drawer. There. Done.

Although...would it hurt to just take a quick peek into Kit's bedroom? I knew exactly where it was, and I was curious to see if it had changed at all over the years. The air was heavy with the sense of being somewhere I shouldn't, but I ignored it and continued down the hall. I paused outside his bedroom door before gently pushing it open.

The walls were painted a light, neutral gray—very different from the little-boy coastal blue he used to have—and he'd added a few modern pieces of Ikea furniture that clashed with the old style of the house. The walls were decorated with vintage ski posters and some framed black and white photographs of snowcapped mountains. On the desk, stuck into a pencil cup, was a purple and green White Mountains Community College pennant. I smiled at the thought of Kit sitting at his desk, doing his homework. I glanced nervously back before moving further into the room. I knew I shouldn't go all the way in, but there was a photograph on the dresser of a young Kit, Riley, and Rebecca—one that I remembered taking at an Autumnboro Halloween Festival—and I wanted a closer look. I picked it up, staring at Kit, and trying to reconcile that face with the one that currently lived here in this house. It was tricky, and I had to look past a bunch of zombie makeup, but it was there. Still him.

I put the photograph down and was about to leave, when a bright pink spiral-bound notebook on the bedside table caught my attention. The thought that it belonged to some woman who'd been frequenting Kit's bedroom—perhaps his Tinder date from the other night?—had me walking over, picking it up, and flipping it open. The first page was blank.

There was still a chance to back out. I shouldn't have even been in Kit's bedroom in the first place. Obviously, whatever was inside that journal was none of my business. The smart thing to do would be to put it down, go back upstairs, and see if Grandpa needed any help.

I turned the page.

On the next page was an exquisitely detailed colored-pencil drawing of our Victorian house. It was decorated as it used to be for autumn with scarecrows sitting on the porch swing and pumpkins cascading down the sides of the steps. I turned the page again to find a close-up sketch of a sign dangling from two chains.

The Autumnboro Inn.

The Autumnboro Inn? My curiosity building, I continued turning pages. As I did, any guilt I'd felt about snooping faded away as each passing sketch began filling me with dread.

"No, no, no, no," I muttered, as the words and drawings started swimming in front of me. A parking lot. A dining room. Guest rooms. A drawing of what looked like Grandpa's collection of White Mountain memorabilia, all displayed in...was that the turret? *My* turret? Below each drawing were notes with question marks—*Load-bearing wall? Commercial-grade kitchen space? Fox unit gutted?*

Fox unit gutted.

Fox. Unit. Gutted.

Gutted.

My stomach turned. These were plans. Plans for turning my beloved family home into some sort of tourist destination! Visions of strangers tromping through the house with dirty boots and ill-mannered children ran through my head. I glanced down at the other books piled on the bedside table. They'd been hidden beneath the journal, but now I could read their titles—*Hospitality Marketing*, *Foundations of Lodging Management*. A sheet of paper was sticking out of one of them, and I pulled it loose. It was a Zillow estimate showing the current value of this property. The current value? Was he insane? I didn't care what Zillow said, this house was priceless!

No wonder he'd been so vague when I'd asked what he was planning to do with his brand-new college degree! He wasn't planning on getting a job at a ski resort. Not here, not in Colorado, not in the South China Sea. No, he was simply biding his time in Autumnboro until Grandpa lost his independence and was forced to move out of this house. My being here—my trying to make sure that Grandpa could stay—was apparently ruining everything. My stomach twisted, and tears stung my eyes.

I thought what had happened between us the other night might have been the beginning of something. Yes, I was planning to go back to Pennsylvania, but I still thought there might be a chance for us. Long distance relationships sometimes worked, right? But, no. I was a fool. All it had been was the goodbye kiss we'd never had. Closure at the end of a lovely day after we had finally cleared the air. I felt so *stupid*. Sneaking in here to see if he'd changed his old bedroom, staring at old photographs. Meanwhile, all Kit cared about was how soon my grandfather and I would be out of his hair so he could get on with his plans.

With shaking hands, I piled everything back on the table and rushed out of the apartment.

CHAPTER 19

"I thought you'd ditched me," Grandpa said, as I burst through the door. He was struggling to get his coat on over his bandaged wrist. "The shuttle will be here any second."

"I'm sorry," I said, helping him with his coat. "I would never ditch you. You know that, right?" I put both my hands on his shoulders and looked him sternly in the eye.

"Sure, sure," he said, looking back at me warily as if I were about to strangle him. He patted my hand as a horn tooted from outside. "That'll be Susan. And, um...like we talked about...Maggie should be over around five."

"No problem," I said. Grandpa and Maggie's love life had suddenly become the least of my concerns. I walked him outside and waved goodbye to the senior center shuttle. I waited until it had circled the common before jogging across the street in the direction of Autumnboro Towing.

I power-walked across the common, fists pumping by my sides, before running out of steam shortly past the funeral home. I slowed down and tried to gather my wits. I needed to be coherent when I confronted Kit with what I'd found. I wasn't sure how I was going to explain what I'd been doing snooping around in his bedroom, but that wasn't a big deal. If he tried to make *that* into the issue, then he was simply attempting to distract me from the fact that his current life goal was to obliterate my ancestral home along with all traces of our shared past. How could he be so heartless?

I finally arrived at the impound lot, scowled at the jumper cable-holding scarecrow etched into the door of the main office, and flung it open. At the clanging of the bells, the man behind the counter looked up from his bagel.

"Can I help you?"

"Kit...Parker," I said, sweating and completely out of breath. "I need...I need to see him."

"You the one who parked on the sidewalk outside Moose's? That'll be one fifty to get it out of impound, and if I were you I'd find myself a good law—"

"What?" I cut in, shaking my head. "No, I didn't park on any sidewalks! I just need to talk to Kit. Is he here?"

"Out back," said the man, looking disappointed and returning to his bagel. "Go ahead."

I walked around back and immediately spotted him, the only human among a sea of cars. Geez. How many people parked illegally in this town? Maybe Grandpa shouldn't feel so bad about driving through Dunkin' Donuts after all.

"Hey!" I shouted.

Kit glanced in my direction, clearly surprised to find me there. He smiled for a brief second before registering the anger in my voice.

"Everything okay?" he asked, wiping his greasy hands on a rag as he walked over to me. He squinted when he saw me up close. "Have you been running?"

"Why don't you tell me if everything is okay?" I asked, ignoring his comment about running because I was, in fact, breathing quite heavily.

"Um..." He turned and looked around the lot. "I thought so. At least on my end. Do you want a water or something?"

"No, I do not want a *water*, Kit. You know what I want? An *explanation*. I want an explanation for the things I saw when I returned your spare key this morning." I nodded emphatically, as if my meaning were obvious.

He winced. "Did Riley answer the door in his underwear again? Geez, Ame, I'm sorry. I told him to stop doing that."

"What?" I shook my head in frustration. "No, Riley wasn't even home! I'm talking about your little pink notebook, Kit! And your little Zillow printout. And all your little guidebooks for turning my home into a tourist trap!" I stepped forward and pushed him hard against the chest.

He took a step back, holding his hands up in the air. "Amy, I can—"

"What?" I interrupted. "You can explain? I'm not an idiot, Kit. I know what I saw!"

"You just said you wanted an explanation!"

"Well, I changed my mind! I know *exactly* what's going on. You want to buy my house and turn it into an inn, or a hotel, or whatever! Correct?"

"Yes, but—"

"And to do that, you need my grandfather to move out. Correct?"

Kit sighed. "*Yes*, but it's not that simple. If you knew—"

"What about all the times I told you why I was here?" I interrupted again. "All the times I told you how much it meant to my grandfather to be able to stay in his home and keep his independence? You never said a word about this! You just stood around agreeing with me while secretly wishing we'd hurry up and *leave*!"

"Amy, that's not—"

"And to top it all off, you want to *gut* the place?" I said, placing my hand over my heart. "How could you even consider that? The Kit I used to know would have never wanted that!"

"Are you finished?" he asked. When I didn't respond, he took a few steps closer, his jaw clenched. Something flashed in his eyes, but when he spoke, it was quite soft. "The Kit you used to know, Amy...the one you knew before you left for college...well, he was still several months away from finding his dead mother's journal."

I froze as his final three words hung in the air. *Dead mother's journal.*

"Oh," I said, my mouth going dry. "I...I had no idea."

I turned around, closed my eyes, and pinched the bridge of my nose. Please tell me I did not just break into this man's house, and then scream at him for keeping his dead mother's journal by his bedside. I did, though. I *so* did.

"A few months after she died," he continued, "my grandmother was going through her things, and she found it. She gave it to me as a keepsake. I had no idea that my mom wanted to open an inn. She'd never mentioned it to any of us. But, according to that journal, it was her dream."

I turned around to face him, tears brimming in my eyes. "And now you want to make it a reality? Now that my grandfather's vulnerable, and his house is in jeopardy, it all seems like perfect timing, huh?"

"I know that house means a lot to your family. Of course I do. But all those ideas in that journal, Amy, they were *hers*. Do you have any idea what making my mom's dream a reality would mean to *me*?"

"So, what then?" I asked. "I go home, and I tell my grandfather that there's been a change of plans? That it's suddenly for the best if we sell the house and put him into assisted living? He just told me"—I swallowed past the lump in my throat. "He just told me that the house is his last connection to my grandmother. He told me this while holding a framed picture of her in his hands, Kit. It was the saddest thing I've ever seen. How can I possibly tell him that he needs to sell?"

"I know," said Kit, raking his hands through his hair. "I know. That's why I hadn't said anything about it yet. To be honest, I don't have enough money to make it happen yet, anyway. My mom's insurance left enough for a down payment, but the renovations will cost a fortune. When you showed up talking about helping Tom stay here longer, I didn't think it was even worth bringing up."

"But you thought it was a good idea to kiss me and lead me on while you waited." I narrowed my eyes. "One last hurrah before you were rid of me."

"I wasn't leading you on. And I certainly don't want to be *rid* of you, Amy. I want...the opposite of that."

"What are you talking about?" I tried to squash down the traitorous feeling of hope that arose in my chest.

"You talk about me leading you on," he said. "What about you? You kissed me back, all while planning on taking off again in a few weeks. How did you think this was going to end?"

I shrugged. "We could've worked something out. Long distance. I don't know. It doesn't matter anymore."

"It does though," he said. "You could make the choice to stay. Sell the house, find a new place for you and your grandfather. They're building some condos just off Main Street. You'd still be in walking distance from the store."

"*Condos?*" I scoffed. "We're going to move into a condo and watch while you tear apart our *home*? Watch while you fill it up with strangers?"

"You think it's better that the three of us keep rattling around in there? Don't you think it would be nice to give new life to the house? Fill it with people who are excited to be there?"

"I don't care about other people," I said, wincing at my own words. "I mean, I usually do. Just not when it comes to this. Don't you even care about all the memories we have there?" I pictured a sledgehammer smashing through my closet in slow motion—fragments of the letters "AEF + KAP" shooting out in every direction.

"If you stay, we can make new memories." He took a step toward me, grabbed my hand, and pressed it against his lips. "And the old ones will always be right here." He moved my hand down to his heart, laying it against his chest.

I rolled my eyes and pulled it out of his grasp. "Even if I wanted to stay and move into some condo, this isn't just about *me*." I took a few steps away, needing space. "We left my grandfather behind because of *my* decision to move. Just because I might be able to make all these awesome new memories, that doesn't mean *he* can. The love of his life is gone, Kit. Just like your mom. Whatever memories they made together, that's all he has for the rest of his life. And once those memories start to fade, he's going to need that house more than ever. Do you think he'll feel safe, and happy, and anchored in some unfamiliar condo?" I shook my head. "No. If I stay, it'll be to make sure that he *never* loses his house."

I turned and walked out of the impound lot, ignoring Kit's pleas for me to come back. To talk about it some more. What else was there to say? Kit and I just weren't meant to be. There was always going to be some sort of obstacle in our way. At least we had resolved our unfinished business that day in the Flume. That was the one positive in all of this. At least this time, when we parted ways, it would be without so much guilt and regret. This time, I'd be able to move on.

CHAPTER 20

The tears came as soon as I'd made it across the street.
Who was I kidding? I would never move on without guilt and regret. I was already feeling the burden of knowing that I was the one stopping Kit from fulfilling his mother's dream. I loved Rebecca, too, but what was I supposed to do? Kit and I couldn't be together if the only reason I moved back to Autumnboro was to thwart his plans. And now that I knew there was a mustache-twirling villain waiting in the wings, I didn't feel right about going back to Pennsylvania, either. Even if I thought Grandpa was going to be okay on his own, one tiny slip and Kit would be there with a construction crew and a wrecking ball. Mom would sell to him in a heartbeat.

No, I had to stay. Grandpa wasn't going to lose his house on my account.

I swiped at my eyes as I turned onto Main Street, plopping down on a bench in front of The Plaid Apple. I needed a few minutes to calm myself down before opening up the store for the day. Just up the street, the door to Jed's General Store swung open and a few bars of peppy ragtime music drifted out from their player piano. I looked around at the mountains and the vibrant trees then down at the pumpkins piled around the base of a nearby tree. It was certainly another beautiful fall day here in Autumnboro. But for the first time since I'd been back, I struggled to appreciate it. Even the ragtime music sounded a bit morose to my ears. As if a skeleton were sitting at the piano, jangling the keys with its bony fingers.

Speaking of which...across the street, the staff of the Shaky Maple had hung Halloween skeletons all across their front window. They were dressed in Shaky Maple T-shirts and aprons, and one of them held a coffee cup in its bony hand, which was funny...I supposed. My sense of humor seemed to have abandoned me. I sighed and took out my phone, searching for a local company that installed motorized stair lifts. I found one and called to make an appointment for a quote the next day. Grandpa wouldn't be thrilled, but he'd just have to accept it if he wanted to stay in his own home. We all had to make sacrifices.

I sat there for a while longer, trying to stop the tears and pull myself together. Trying to think of more things I could do to Grandpa-proof the house. Locks on the kitchen cabinets? No, that was for toddlers. Surely Grandpa wasn't going to drink a bottle of Drano? How about a seat inside the shower? Yes, that was one! I typed *shower seat* into a note on my phone. Although, Grandpa didn't even have a real shower. He used an old clawfoot tub that had been converted into a shower about a million years ago. I wasn't even sure if you could fit a seat inside it. I closed the note and instead googled *ways to make home safe for old people*.

Install raised toilet seat.

I laughed out loud at the look on Grandpa's face if I ever attempted that one. My sense of humor seemed to be returning, which was a good sign. I blew my nose and continued down the list. *Remove locks from bedroom doors. Install video monitors.* I shuddered at the thought of Grandpa having Maggie over tonight. No and no. *Widen doorframes and hallways.* The doorframes and hallways in our old house were certainly narrow. If he needed to use a wheelchair someday, it would never fit. *Install ramps for entering and exiting the home*. If he was in a wheelchair someday, he'd definitely need those ramps, too.

Which meant that we would also need to retrofit his bathroom. That clawfoot shower tub was definitely not handicap accessible. I scanned the list until I came to *install a walk-in bathtub*. I clicked the link, which brought me to the website for Home Depot, laughing out loud again when I saw the prices. Okay, maybe I should just start with the stair lift and go from there. Grandpa would need to be eased into the rest of this stuff, anyway. One thing at a time. Feeling a bit better, I put my phone away and turned around to check my reflection in the window of The Plaid Apple.

"What the—"

I gasped at the sight of what had been behind me the entire time. Lining the windowsills of The Plaid Apple were pumpkin candles, pumpkin knickknacks, and big sacks full of pumpkin-flavored coffee. Stuck to the glass were an assortment of pumpkin decals and gel clings. I turned around to see if anybody else was seeing this and noticed the chalkboard sign that had been placed out on the sidewalk:

Now Selling Pumpkin Everything!
50% Off!
Best Deals in Town!

Seriously? I flung open the door and marched inside. Jackie was there behind the counter, pouring coffee for Moose. She looked up briefly at the wild clanging of the bells, saw who it was, and looked away again.

"What's with all the pumpkin stuff?" I asked, walking up to

the counter and motioning toward the windows. "Are you trying to put my grandfather out of business?"

She shrugged and placed the coffeepot back on the burner. "Thought I'd branch out a little. Apples are a bit, what's the word, Moose?"

"Tacky," said Moose, a strip of bacon dangling between his lips.

"Tacky, that's right," said Jackie. "Kind of like...oh, I don't know....*blueberries?*"

I winced. She'd gone and read one of my books. She'd actually done it. And she'd clearly chosen *Nightmare in the North* where the blueberry-themed local restaurant was described as tacky, kitschy, and—I cringed as my own words came back to haunt me—straight out of the eighties. Orion had loved that description. Orion had *come up* with that description, after I'd shown him pictures of Kit, Riley, and me goofing around behind the counter of The Plaid Apple when we were kids. Jackie had been wearing one of her biker T-shirts, bangs spiked to the heavens.

"Jackie, look," I said, squeezing myself between Moose and the man beside him, whom I quickly recognized as Donnie from the auto shop. "The Striped Blueberry is a fictitious restaurant! It has *nothing* to do with this place! They serve blueberries! You serve apples! It's like the old saying—*you can't compare apples to blueberries.*"

"Don't you mean oranges?" asked some random guy at the counter. I shot him a look, and he went back to his breakfast.

Jackie put her hands on her hips and glowered at me through heavily mascaraed eyes. "Tell me again how many people got food poisoning from that blueberry cobbler? Was it...*the entire town*? Get you two some more bacon?" She smiled sweetly at Moose and Donnie before heading back into the kitchen.

I wanted to follow after her. I wanted to ask her not to take out her anger with me on my innocent grandfather's store. But going into the kitchen would probably violate some health codes and make things even worse. Besides, I was sort of trapped there between Moose and Donnie.

"Hey, guys," I said, forcing a smile as I attempted to dislodge myself. "Long time, no see?" Neither of them smiled back.

"You know," said Moose, taking a loud slurp of his coffee, "I, too, have read one of your books. Donnie here suggested one the other day. Thought I might find it interesting."

"Sure did," said Donnie.

"Oh, that's nice," I said, as a fresh wave of dread hit my stomach. I shimmied free from between the two men and smoothed out my coat. "I appreciate that. Any update on my car, Donnie? By any chance?"

Donnie let out a long, deep belly laugh before returning to his pancakes.

"You know what my favorite part of that book was?" asked Moose, swiveling around on his stool to face me. I hadn't looked at Moose head-on in years. His long brown beard was tinged with gray, and he'd put on quite a bit of weight. He was looking more like his namesake than ever.

"The ending?" I guessed. There was still a chance that he'd actually enjoyed the book. I held out hope, even as my stomach dropped to around knee level. "The happy ending where all is forgiven and nobody holds a grudge?"

"Nope. I liked the part where that nimrod plows his police cruiser into some animal on his first day on the job. Remember that? Remember how he spends the rest of his career as the laughingstock of the police force? What was his nickname again? Bear? Bull?"

I took a few more steps until I had reached the door, gripping the handle for dear life. With my safety net in place, I looked Moose right in his moosey little eyes.

"Buck," I said clearly, keeping my head held high. "I believe his nickname was Buck."

At that, I gave the door a shove, only for it to shudder and not budge an inch. Orion was totally right about this place being straight out of the eighties. With a determined ram of my shoulder, the door burst open, and I hurried outside. The sound of Moose and Donnie's raucous laughter followed me all the way up the sidewalk and onto the doorstep of Pumpkin Everything. I quickly unlocked the door and slipped inside, closing it firmly behind me.

Now that thoughts of Orion were once again front and center in my mind, the onslaught of pumpkin spice that surrounded me was highly unpleasant. I slid to the floor, my back against the door, and tried my hardest not to breathe.

CHAPTER 21

An hour later, and still restless from my assorted angry confrontations with pretty much the entire town, I spotted Riley through the front window. He was heading up the street—head down, staring at his phone—and into the Shaky Maple. Even though I'd been expecting it, his cold reception had been hanging over me all week. Just because I was currently angry with his brother, didn't mean that I didn't want to try to patch things up with Riley. And if a heart-to-heart over coffee didn't do the trick, I would just have to console myself with the fact that I hadn't written mean things about him in any of my books.

I taped a *Back in Fifteen Minutes* sign to the door and ran across the street. Riley was there at the end of the line, a black hooded sweatshirt thrown over his button-up shirt and dress pants. I nudged him with my elbow to get his attention.

"Buy you a coffee?" I asked after he'd looked up and pulled out his earphones.

He looked down at me cautiously. "Sure."

I glanced around the coffee shop as we waited silently in line. The Shaky Maple hadn't changed. It still had its cozy, exposed brick walls, mismatched tables, and enormous antler chandelier. The mural of a multicolored maple tree was still there, painted across the back wall, and a large selection of seasonal lattes was still written in colorful chalk letters on a board behind the counter. *Pumpkin spice latte.* It was funny, but if it weren't for my reminder of Orion earlier, I could have almost gone for one. We reached the front of the line, ordered our drinks, and found a table by the window.

"You're special, you know?" I said, popping the lid off my coffee to help cool it down. "You're the only person in town mad at me for something other than my books."

Riley took a long sip of his drink—some frozen concoction called a Maple Sugar Crush—his dark eyes boring into mine. I looked away, following the frozen coffee as it moved up his straw. "Is that so?"

I nodded. "You're equally justified, though. Don't get me wrong."

"You think I'm mad at you?"

I raised my eyebrows. "Aren't you?"

Riley placed his drink down on the table and shoved his hands into his sweatshirt pockets. "You know, I never minded being the third wheel," he said after a moment.

"Third wheel?"

"To you and Kit." He tipped his chair casually back on two legs, looking out the window. "There was always something going on between the two of you, and I was just the annoying little brother. That made me a third wheel."

"That's not true," I protested, but Riley shook his head.

"It is. But like I said, I didn't mind." He looked down at his drink, slowly rocking his chair, and avoiding eye contact. "You were like an older sister to me, Amy. I idolized the both of you. I was just happy that you never told me to get lost."

"And you were like a little brother to *me*," I said, leaning forward, trying to catch his eye. "I loved having you around, Riley. I always did."

"And yet you left without saying goodbye to your *little brother*." He air-quoted the words, finally meeting my eyes as his chair thudded back down to the ground. "You couldn't even find the time to explain to me why you were leaving."

"I'm sorry," I said lamely. "It wasn't on purpose."

We looked at each other, silently, for a few seconds.

"I was never *mad* at you," he said at last. "Not really. Just hurt...and confused. Did you really think Kit, in the state he was in, was going to bother explaining anything to me? After you left, Gram and I could barely get five words out of him."

"I'm sorry," I said again, reaching across the table for his hand, which he quickly drew away. I leaned back, dropping my hand into my lap.

"I didn't mind being the third wheel," he repeated, looking out the window. "But when you left like that...I realized that maybe you'd never told me to get lost because you'd never even noticed I was there."

"That's not true," I said, tears stinging my eyes. "Look at me." He reluctantly pulled his eyes away from the window. "You were the *best* kid, Riley. None of this had anything to do with you. I wasn't thinking, that was all. I spent those last few months before college in a daze of self-preservation, doing nothing but trying to avoid Kit. I never meant for that to include you. I was just so laser focused on getting away from Autumnboro as soon as possible that it just sort of...happened."

"So, I was collateral damage?" he asked, his eyes boring into me again. Talk about laser focused.

"You were collateral damage," I admitted. "And I'm so, so sorry."

His intense gaze softened a bit. "You know, I'd already lost my dad. That year it felt like I'd lost my mother, my brother, and my sister, too. All at once." He sank back into his chair and took a moody sip from his drink. "It sucked."

"I'm sorry," I said, reaching across the table for his hand again. This time he pulled it from his pocket and let me take it. How could I not have considered how alone he must have felt with his mother gone and Kit being so withdrawn? My chest tightened as I squeezed his hand. "But if you'll let me...I'd really like another chance to be your big sister again."

A trace of a smile appeared at the corner of his mouth. "Maybe we could work something out. Although, you're leaving again in a few weeks, aren't you?"

"Maybe not," I said, letting go of his hand. "The last time I left, I was a self-centered teenager. I did the same thing to my grandfather that I did to you. I left without even bothering to tell him why, and I've been living with the guilt ever since. Now might be the perfect time to start making up for it."

"So, is that why you came back? Guilt?"

"Pretty much."

"Did you make out with Kit out of guilt, too?"

My jaw dropped. "Were you *spying* on us?"

"I may have tripped over a shoe and fallen through the front curtains. Anything I saw after that...wasn't my fault."

"Maybe you should stop staring at that thing so much." I pointed to his phone on the table. "And no, I didn't kiss your brother out of guilt. It's already over, anyway. I found out this morning that he wants to turn our house into a Disney resort."

"I'd call it more of a country B&B."

"So, you know?"

"It'd be sort of weird if I didn't. She was my mom, too."

I slumped back in my chair. "You're cool with the house being destroyed, then? With all the memories you have of growing up there being reduced to...well....memories?"

"I love that house," he said. "But the memories we made,

they'll always be up here." He tapped a finger against the side of his head, reminding me of Kit.

"That's not enough for me," I said. "And it definitely won't be enough for my grandfather someday."

"What do you mean?"

"Um, Alzheimer's...dementia...."

"Tom has Alzheimer's?" Riley leaned forward, his eyebrows raised in concern.

"No, of course not. I mean, not yet. Hopefully never. But who knows? If the time ever does come, I want him to be in a home he's familiar with."

"And what does your grandfather think about this?"

"I haven't told him yet." I sighed. "But he's already told me that the house is his last connection to my grandmother. Doesn't that say it all?"

"You don't think he'd feel differently if he knew the inn would be honoring my mom?"

"He probably would," I admitted. Grandpa had always been fond of Rebecca. "He'd probably agree to sell out of guilt, and I don't want him to do that."

"You realize there's a difference between doing something out of guilt and doing something out of love, right?"

"Of course I—"

I was interrupted by an alert from Riley's phone. He picked it up, aimed it into the corner of the coffee shop, and started tapping rapidly at the screen.

"Pikachu," he said, flipping the phone around so I could see. I rolled my eyes as a second alert went off.

"Jigglypuff?"

"I wish. But no. I have a meeting in twenty minutes that I forgot about. I should probably get back to work."

"You really like being a funeral planner?" I asked as we gathered up our things and walked toward the door. "All death, all the time?" I waved my hands spookily in the air.

He snorted. "It's not like that."

"What *is* it like?"

"It's like..." He paused and looked off into the distance. "It's like I'm giving people a little bit of control over something that none of us can control. At least that's how I think about it."

I nodded, thoughtfully. "Whatever it is, I'm proud of you." I reached up to give him a hug, relieved beyond belief when he leaned down and hugged me firmly back.

"I'm proud of you, too," he said. "I've been meaning to read those books of yours. I just haven't had the time."

"Right." I laughed, gently pushing him through the door. "Don't do me any favors. I'll see you later, Riley. Thanks for the talk."

"You, too. I'll see you later, Ame."

With a smile and a wave, he flicked up his hood and took off down the sidewalk—head down, staring at his phone.

CHAPTER 22

Later that evening, I watched from our living room window as a van from Winter's Eve Assisted Living pulled into the driveway, Josie's bright red Tesla trailing closely behind. Josie, being a total saint, had invited me to spend the night at her house in order to give Grandpa and Maggie their privacy.

"You don't *have* to go," said Maggie, dropping two bags of Chinese food on the kitchen table. She pulled my coat off the back of a chair and tossed it to me, replacing it with her own. "There's plenty of food." She turned and gave Grandpa a frisky wink.

"Nope!" I said, grabbing my overnight bag from the floor. "I'm good. Josie's waiting. You guys have fun!" I pulled Grandpa quickly aside before leaving, giving him strict orders not to do anything that might further injure his wrist. Then I gave myself strict orders to forget that I ever said such a thing.

Josie's house wasn't far, and while it was definitely luxurious, it was smaller than I'd expected. It was a log cabin-style home, set right on the Pemigewasset River. The entire back of the house was lined with windows and a wraparound porch.

"It's actually pretty terrifying when it gets dark outside," she said as we sipped wine after dinner, watching *The Great British Baking Show* on her eighty-two-inch flat screen. "At night, I usually just hide upstairs."

As the sun went down, and the windows became a solid panel of looming blackness, I saw her point. When the episode ended, we moved into the kitchen. There was probably nothing out there to worry about, other than a few wild animals. Although, the Wolfman from Clark's Trading Post did cross my mind along with a vision of his grizzly face pressed up against the glass. I shuddered and took a seat at the breakfast bar, facing away from the windows. Josie busied herself with warming up a coffee cake she'd ordered from QVC.

"Is there anything your mom doesn't sell?" she asked, popping the cake into the oven. "I get these on auto-delivery every ninety days. Of course, I can't eat that many, so," she threw open the freezer to reveal a stack of boxes, "just another thing for me to hand out around town."

I smiled as I topped off my wine. "You're quite the philanthropist."

As we ate dessert, I filled her in on everything I'd learned that morning about Kit's plans for the house.

"So, let me get this straight," she said. "The love of your life wants to buy the house you guys both grew up in, but you'll only let that happen over your dead body. And if he somehow does manage to buy it, he doesn't actually have enough money to make the renovations?"

"Right," I said. "But whether or not he has the money isn't the point. The point is that he wants to do this. He's being completely heartless."

"But it's for his mom, soooo...."

"So *what*?"

Josie looked at me like I was nuts. "So he's sort of the opposite of heartless, isn't he? A man whose goal in life is to fulfill his mother's dying wish? That's kind of the sweetest thing ever."

"It wasn't her *dying wish*," I nitpicked. "It was just some drawings in a notebook." I felt a pang of guilt as I reduced Rebecca's plans down to "some drawings in a notebook." But it wasn't like she'd made a deathbed declaration of intent or anything. Kit had even said himself that he wasn't sure how serious she'd been about it.

"Well, whatever it is," said Josie, "it's obviously important to Kit. Are you sure you want to end your relationship over something so...selfless?"

"First of all, there is no relationship. When we started something the other night, it was without me having all the information I needed to make an informed decision." I stabbed my fork into a second piece of cake before pulling it out again and pointing it at Josie. "And, in case you forgot, I'm trying to save the house for my grandfather. Is that not an equally selfless act? Why am I the bad guy?"

"But don't you think it would be amazing to work at a B&B?" she asked, ignoring my question and twirling around on her stool. "New people to talk to every day? It'd be like you were traveling the world without ever having to leave home. You'd never be alo—" She stopped in the middle of her sentence, her eyes suddenly focusing on something behind me, her face registering an expression of total surprise.

"What?" I asked, panic rising in my chest. I spun around to face the windows, preparing myself to find the Wolfman, or Pennywise, or maybe just a run-of-the-mill psychotic murderer. But there was nothing there. I looked at Josie. "What is it?"

"I've just had the most fantastic idea."

"Oh?"

She nodded and placed a hand on her chest. "I could invest in the B&B. I've got loads of money!"

"Oh," I repeated, my stomach dropping. "And, um, what B&B might that be?" I gave her a pointed death stare.

"The one that Kit wants to...oh, right. Over your dead body." She cleared her throat and slid down off the stool. "More wine?"

"You'd be cool with yanking an old man's house out from under him just because it might be fun to work at a B&B?" I called after her. "Is that what you're telling me?"

"Not when you put it *that* way," she said. "Geez. But, you know, you could always stay in Autumnboro and find a place with a nice in-law apartment. If you had one of those, you wouldn't need to seek alternate accommodations every time Tom had a *guest* over." She air-quoted the word and gave me a wink. "Then, you know, you and Kit could get on with it."

"Get on with it?"

"Marriage. Babies. What are you, thirty?"

"Twenty-eight," I said through gritted teeth.

"Right. You're twenty-eight—closing in on thirty—and you've got this amazing second chance with a handsome guy, who wants to spend his life honoring his mother who died tragically young. You're willing to give that up over some old house?"

"I just don't want to make any more selfish decisions," I said, swirling the remnants of my wine around the bottom of my glass. "That's what selling feels like to me. When I was a teenager, I left town to get away from Kit. Now, I'm going to sell the house in order to come back and be with him? No matter what I do, my poor grandfather always seems to lose."

Josie refilled my wine and put a piece of foil over the small leftover hunk of coffee cake. "Maybe you should ask him," she said, glancing up and smiling at me sympathetically. "Your grandfather, I mean. Maybe you should ask him if having you stay, and seeing you happy, would really feel like losing."

CHAPTER 23

Josie and I spent the next day together at the store. At four o'clock, I left her in charge of closing up, while I went home to meet a representative from Sunshine Stair Lifts. His name was Ray, and he spent about thirty seconds looking at the stairs before scribbling some numbers on a yellow slip of paper. In total silence, he folded it and handed it to me, like we were negotiating a seven-figure legal settlement.

"Five grand?" I asked, my eyes widening. Maybe he'd written it down because he wasn't able to say the number out loud without laughing.

"Give or take."

I blew out a breath. Wow. That was way more than I thought it would be. That was even more than a walk-in bathtub. But it was for Grandpa's safety, and that was all that mattered, right?

"Okay," I said. "I mean, not *okay* okay. Don't start ordering parts or anything. I need to think it over. Run it past my mother." I cringed at the thought of calling Mom with an estimate like this. She'd probably tell Isaac Mizrahi and they'd both have a good laugh over it. At the sound of the senior center shuttle arriving outside, I opened the front door and waved to Susan as she helped Grandpa down the steps. She looked over at me, but rather than waving back, reached up and scratched her forehead with her middle finger.

Oh.

Was that...was that on *purpose*? Somewhat disconcerted, I stepped aside to let Grandpa into the front hall.

"Hello, hello," he said as I kissed him on the cheek. He gave Ray a suspicious glance. "Who's this?"

"This is Ray," I said. "He works for Sunshine Stair Lifts." I annunciated each word, trying to make it sound shiny and fun as I fanned out the stack of pamphlets Ray had given me. On each of the covers was a smiling white-haired person, happily seated in their exorbitantly-priced lift, riding up a flight of sparkling white stairs, totally free from fear of breaking a hip.

Grandpa grimaced. "No way."

"What do you mean, *no way*? These chairs are designed to help people stay in their homes *longer*. Isn't that what we want?"

"How much do these contraptions cost?"

I handed him the slip of paper and he burst out laughing. I smiled apologetically at Ray who'd started gathering up his things.

"Hang on a minute," said Grandpa. He walked over to the hall table, scribbled the words NO WAY on the same slip of paper, and handed it back to Ray. Still laughing, he continued on his way up the stairs.

"Give me a call when you've made a decision," said Ray, rolling his eyes and opening the front door.

"Okay, thanks!" I called over my shoulder, following Grandpa up the stairs. I closed the apartment door behind us and looked him sternly in the face. "We need to talk." I walked over to the couch and patted the cushions. He shuffled over and down beside me.

"If this is about that contraption, you can forget it," said Grandpa.

"It's not about th—"

"TIME FOR YOUR MEDICATION! PRESS BUTTON TO DISPENSE! TIME FOR YOUR MEDICATION! PRESS BUTTON TO DISPENSE!"

I put my head in my hands as we were interrupted by the Medi-Magic 3000 going off like a banshee from the kitchen. "Go on," I said. "Take your pills before that thing calls Mom on us."

When he returned, I came right out and told him that Kit wanted to buy the house. I told him all about the journal I'd found and about Rebecca's dream of turning the house into The Autumnboro Inn. He listened to all of it with an expression that I couldn't quite read.

"She always was very creative," he said when I'd finished. "Always restoring those antiques. Such a warm person, too. She would have been wonderful at running an inn."

"She would have," I agreed. Kit had that same warmth. Imagine walking into an inn to find someone like him behind the check-in desk? What a way to start your getaway. I couldn't imagine a single negative Yelp review. "But, still," I continued, shaking away the image that had almost made me smile. "This is our *home*. We can't just let him knock down walls, and rip out floors, and open the whole place up to strangers! There are memories everywhere I look! Over there is where Kit and I sat in front of the fireplace to play Chinese checkers. And over there," I pointed to the corner of the living room, "is where we practiced our performance for the middle school talent show."

"Now there's a memory I could stand to lose," muttered Grandpa.

"I'm being serious," I said, lightly slapping him on the knee. "I've decided that if Kit's going to act like a ghoulish vulture, waiting around to grab this house just as soon as you're down on your luck, then I'm going to make sure that your luck never runs out. If I move back in, and we install a stair lift, and a few other," I cleared my throat, "minor modifications, then we can keep this house forever."

"Forever, huh?"

"You got a problem with forever?"

He shrugged. "You would really move back in here just to keep him from making his mother's dream come true?"

"*No,*" I said, hating the way he made it sound. Whose side was he on, anyway? "I would move back here because you told me that this house is your last connection to Gram. And because if I hadn't run off back in high school, Mom and Dad might still be living here and none of this would be happening."

"So you're willing to give up your future to fix the past?" asked Grandpa, narrowing his eyes. "Did I just end up in an episode of *Doctor Who*?"

"What future am I giving up?" I asked. "Orion's gone. There's nothing for me in Pennsylvania. I can write my books here in the turret, and I can work part-time at the store with you and Josie. It sounds like the ideal future to me."

"I wasn't talking about that fool you almost married. I'm talking about—" He pointed down at the floor.

"What about him?"

"I may have tripped over a cord and fallen through the front curtains the other night. I couldn't help but see you two smooching it up on the porch."

I pinched the bridge of my nose and closed my eyes. Apparently, everybody in the house had watched us that night. "Whatever that was, it's over now. And it's definitely over once I move back in with you. Once buying the house is off the table, I don't see why he'd stick around. He'll probably move out and open an inn somewhere else. Or get a job at a resort in some other state." I shrugged.

Grandpa nodded and tapped at the pamphlets I was still holding in my lap. "What's next after this? A crane to lift me into bed? Maybe I can start riding to the senior center by ambulance?"

"You're a funny, funny old man," I said, sinking back against the pillows and avoiding his question. Now was apparently not the time to bring up the walk-in bathtub.

"And you're a good girl," said Grandpa, picking up the remote and turning on the TV. *Sharyn's Closet* was in full swing. "You've got some crazy ideas in your head, but you're a good girl."

I gave him a smile, and we sat there companionably, watching my mother sell denim jackets and platform flip-flops until it was time for dinner.

CHAPTER 24

Over the next few days, Josie was kind enough to chauffeur us around to Grandpa's doctor's appointments, the grocery store, and anywhere else we needed to be. While she seemed genuinely happy to help, I really did need to get my car back. The last I'd heard from Donnie, he'd sent it over to a buddy of his in North Conway for a second opinion. Which, if we're being honest, probably meant that he'd abandoned it behind Walmart.

I'd also come to the conclusion that Susan Blake, having followed through on her promise to read one of my books, had most definitely flipped me the bird. While she hadn't made the gesture since that day, she did continue to snub all my smiles and friendly waves. Jackie was still passive-aggressively selling pumpkin merchandise at the diner, and Moose continued giving me a daily dose of stink-eye whenever I passed by the mini mart. Even our pizza deliveries had been taking over an hour to arrive, thanks to Autumnboro Baller, Mike.

The townsfolk were gathering their pitchforks, and I needed to find a way to make amends. Especially if I wanted to move back here permanently. But what could I do? Pull my books off

Amazon? Writing was my livelihood, and those books had taken me years of hard work. Besides, I hadn't actually written them out of malice. Sure, it *seemed* that I had. And yes, the parts that Orion had influenced were a bit mean-spirited and snide. But at the heart of it, this town and the people in it were so memorable that even though I'd gone away, they'd never been forgotten. They were true characters, and I didn't see that as such a bad thing. If only I could make them see it that way, too.

* * *

I WOKE up early on Saturday morning, assuming that Grandpa was still asleep in his bed, and went into the turret to attempt to get some writing done. I'd awoken that morning with an idea for a spin-off series. It would still be set in Fallsburg, Vermont, with the same cast of characters, only, instead of gory horror, I was thinking…cozy mystery. Perhaps my characters had learned from their past mistakes. Perhaps Susan's character, the town gossip, had learned to use her affliction for good and taken to solving murders like Miss Marple. Perhaps Moose's counterpart, after spending years as the laughingstock of the police force, could emerge the unlikely hero. The underdog that everybody had been secretly rooting for all along. Without Orion around to bring out the worst in me, I thought that I could make it work. I typed for over an hour, the words flowing easily for the first time in months, only stopping at the sound of my phone buzzing a text alert.

Kit.

That wasn't unusual. He'd been texting me all week with things like *We need to talk* or *You're overreacting.* I usually ignored him or texted back a poop emoji. This one, however, was different.

Please come outside.

Come outside? I peeked through the curtains but didn't see anything.

Why?

I waited as the three little dots blinked at me, resisting the urge to fire off a poop emoji. And then...

Just come out.

I rolled my eyes. Fine. If he wanted to get into an argument in the middle of the front lawn, why not? The neighbors should probably get used to it. Someday they might witness me chaining myself to the front porch, shouting my protest at a line of oncoming bulldozers. I put on my coat, skipped down the stairs, and stepped outside. Nothing. My phone buzzed again.

Around back.

I walked around to the backyard where I found Grandpa, Susan Blake, and what looked like the entire over-sixty-five population of Autumnboro. There were several folding tables set up, including one filled with donuts, coffee, and apple cider. Old clothing, shoes, and hats were strewn all over the grass, along with burlap sacks and rakes. I put a hand over my mouth when I realized what was going on, barely registering the fact that Susan was scratching her forehead at me again.

"Scarecrows?" I called out to Riley, standing by the donuts. I refused to make eye contact with Kit, whom I sensed watching me from the back porch.

He raised his coffee cup in the air. "The tradition has been resurrected! Only, my brother turned it into some sort of elderly get-together, and Tom can't actually do anything one-handed."

"It's called Scarecrows for Seniors," snapped Barbara Cortland, coming over and pinching Riley on the elbow. "And it was a wonderful idea. Tom's here for moral support, he doesn't need to do a thing. The rest of us," she gave me a pointed look, "are going to stuff as many scarecrows as we can so Kit can deliver them to people who need some cheering up."

"That's so sweet," I said, trying to ignore the look she was giving me. She'd definitely read *Bad Reception.* I could see it in her eyes. They were filled with fresh memories of that chapter in which she punishes all the students by forcing them to—

No. I couldn't even think about it without feeling like a total monster. I took a few steps back, bracing myself for impact as she marched toward me with her fuchsia lips pursed.

"You going to get out here and help, or what?" she snapped. "Do some *good* for this town for a change?"

"Oh," I said, taken aback that she hadn't pile driven me straight into the tomato plants. "Of course! I definitely want to do some good. I would love to make up for anything I may have said, or done, or...or written...that was, you know...*wrong.*" Our eyes locked as the word hung heavily in the air. Then she gave me a brisk nod and took off back to her table. I let out a breath of relief. Wow. Okay. Terrifying Barbara Cortland was more forgiving than the rest of this town. Who would've guessed?

Feeling encouraged, I took off across the yard toward Grandpa when my foot came down on something pointy and unstable. Somebody grabbed me by the elbow and pushed me aside.

"You almost took your eye out," said Kit, grabbing the rake I'd nearly stepped on. I plucked it from his hand, my eyes sweeping down to his New England Patriots sweatshirt. At a sudden loss for words, I said the first thing that came into my mind.

"I'm a Steelers fan now. So...your sweatshirt...I think it really stinks!" I spun around like a two-year-old and stormed off across the yard. Nice one.

"Amy!" he called after me. "Come back here. Please. I want to talk."

Reluctantly, I came to a halt, rolled my eyes, and turned around.

"You planned all this?" I asked, glancing around the yard, trying to act cool. Trying to act as if this whole thing meant nothing to me, when in reality, I wanted to burst into tears.

Stuffing scarecrows was my favorite childhood memory, and the heartless jerk had gone and resurrected it.

He nodded. "It's a Senior Citizens Council thing. It's one of our new fall events."

"New, huh?"

He shrugged and gave me a small smile. "The idea came to me very, very recently. On the side of a scenic highway, I think it was."

I fought the urge to stand on my tiptoes and kiss him. I wanted to tell him that this meant the world to me and that I couldn't have imagined a more perfect way to spend a fall morning. Instead, I looked over to where Maggie was feeding Grandpa a donut, lovingly wiping powder off his upper lip, and strengthened my resolve.

"If you have your way," I said, "I suppose this will be the last time anyone stuffs a scarecrow around here, huh?"

"I want to open an inn, Amy, not a strip mall. There would still be scarecrow stuffing. There'd be all kinds of family activities, actually." His eyes lit up as he spoke, and for a moment I was looking at a teenaged Kit again—scoping out motels on Route 3, filled with boundless optimism. For a moment I saw how much this meant to him.

"Well, I'm sure that will be lovely for the *tourists*," I said, shoving away my sympathy. "And screw the rest of us." I turned and walked briskly up the back steps. Kit followed me.

"Don't go inside," he said. "Please. I want you to enjoy this, whether it's the last time or not."

"*Not.*"

"Have you even tried to see any of this from my perspective?" he asked. "And when I say that, I don't mean my perspective that you've made up in your head where I look like a comic-book villain. I mean my *actual* perspective? The one where this inn would be in honor of my mother? My mother who you loved— and who loved you back like one of her own?"

"Are you trying to guilt me into agreeing to this?"

"No," he said. "Of course not. I just want you to realize that this isn't some heartless, evil plan of mine. I mean, I never expected to see you again, Amy. I stopped waiting for you to come back a long, long time ago. Why would I even think that this house still meant anything to you?"

"Well it *does*," I said, adamantly. "And even if it didn't, what about my grandfather? You didn't think about him at all!"

"Have you even talked to him about this yet?"

"Sort of," I said, as Grandpa's words came back to me. *You'd give up your future, to fix the past?* "Briefly." I didn't want to give Kit the idea that Grandpa might, in any way, be okay with selling.

"Hey, Kit! Stop your flirting and get back to work!" A chorus of laughter erupted as a straw hat sailed onto the back porch, landing between us.

"Be right there!" he called, tossing the hat back like a Frisbee. "Can we talk about this later? For now...truce?"

I sighed. Obviously, I wanted to dig my hands into those crunchy leaves, and sink my teeth into an apple cider donut, rather than go back, alone, into the house to wallow in guilt and self-doubt. There'd be plenty of time for that later.

"Fine," I said. "Truce."

CHAPTER 25

"—And then I said, 'Those aren't pillows!'"

Everyone seated at the table burst out laughing as Walter delivered his punch line. My spirits had lifted considerably as we all set to work gathering leaves and stuffing them into shirts and pants, pausing every now and then to shake some over an unsuspecting person's head. As Kit, Riley, Grandpa, Maggie, Barbara, Walter, Evelyn, and I sewed faces onto burlap sacks, the conversation ranged from television shows to town gossip to decades' worth of Autumnboro memories.

I hadn't realized that Maggie and Grandpa had known each other since they were kids, or that Walter had been a volunteer firefighter, or that Evelyn had been a local talk radio personality. The conversation eventually turned to the annual Halloween festival. Every year, for the week leading up to Halloween, people poured in from all over the country to experience the holiday in the Autumn Capital of the World. I sensed Kit's eyes on me at the mention of the festival, and I quickly busied myself with stuffing a chambray shirt sleeve.

I wondered if he was remembering the same thing as me.

We'd been fourteen. I was in a puffy black coat, cat ears, and tail, and Kit had been dressed as the cutest Han Solo I'd ever seen. We'd just been through the haunted house inside Town Hall and were holding hands as we spilled outside, laughing. I'd grabbed his hand when a zombie jumped out from behind the town clerk's desk, and he hadn't let go. We'd run straight onto the common, trailed by Riley, and collapsed onto the grass behind a towering display of jack-o'-lanterns. We stared up at their warm, flickering glow, and at the stars beyond, while we lay there, catching our breath.

The memory was magical, and despite the current cruddy circumstances, I was happy that I'd be around this year for the festival. I wouldn't be holding hands and gazing up at the stars with Kit, but hanging out with Josie and Grandpa could be fun, too.

By lunchtime, there were more than thirty scarecrows lined up along the front porch, dressed in a colorful hodgepodge of flannel shirts, patched-up jeans, and straw hats. Kit was going to drop each one off personally later in the afternoon. As the last person left, and Maggie disappeared into the house with Grandpa, Kit and I were left alone outside. I held a trash bag open as he swept away the last of the coffee cups and napkins, sneaking glances at him as we worked together in silence. My heart ached with the unfairness of it all. I could have so easily seen us doing this sort of mundane task together all the time. Cleaning up after holidays, birthday parties, and weeknight dinners. Why we lived in a constant state of trash collection, I wasn't sure. But the visual was nice. I dropped the trash bag into a barrel and went off to gather up the rakes, thinking.

Rebecca would have understood why The Autumnboro Inn could never be built here. Sure, the house and the location were perfect for it, but she also knew that this was the Fox family's *home*. She never would have wanted Grandpa to have to move out. Or me and Kit to end up fighting over it. Perhaps those drawings had just been a hobby, like a dollhouse or a fairy garden, that Kit was taking way too seriously. I wondered how long he would stay here once buying the house was off the table. A year? A few months? I supposed once he moved out, Riley would follow. The house was convenient to his job at the funeral home, but he really didn't need such a large space all to himself. He would probably find a small studio apartment, and eventually, new tenants would move in.

Tenants.

The Parkers weren't tenants, they were family. But if they left, then yes, we'd have tenants. Strangers. The unpleasant thought was followed quickly by another, more unsettling one. Would keeping the house be worth it, if Kit wasn't in it?

Yes. Of *course*, it would be.

Grandpa wasn't in love with Kit. What did it matter to him whether the Parkers stayed or not? His connection to this house was about his memories with Gram, and his children, and me. Whoever happened to live downstairs was irrelevant to him. Maybe it wasn't irrelevant to *me*, but it was to him; and I needed to keep my priorities straight.

"Heads up," said Kit, pulling me out of my thoughts.

I looked up as a cloud of dry brown leaves rained down over my head.

Kit stood laughing on the back deck as I plucked the crunchy bits out of my hair and brushed them off my coat.

"Are you serious?" I asked, scooping a handful off the ground and running up the back steps. He ducked out of the way as I flung them at him, and a sudden breeze blew most of them back into my face.

"Nice try, Fox." He laughed, taking off down the steps and into the yard. I ran after him, going for the big mountain of leaves piled against the fence—the ones that were black and damp and hopefully full of bugs. Protected by my coat and gloves, I scooped up an armful and flung them right into his face.

"That better?" I asked.

"Oh, you're dead," he said, still laughing as he wiped soggy leaves out of his nose and mouth. He took off after me as I ran out of our yard and across the street to the common. I glanced back to find him with one of the scarecrows draped across his shoulders in a fireman's carry. Laughing and out of breath, I stopped when I came to the playground. I grabbed the tire swing and held it in front of me like a shield.

"What are you doing with that?" I asked. "Riley made that one."

"He won't mind." He reached into the scarecrow's chest, Temple of Doom style, and started yanking out handfuls of leaves. I let out a small scream, ducking and bobbing behind the tire as he flung them at me. Then I shoved the swing at him and took off toward the house, going straight for the garden hose. I turned around, aiming it at him.

"You would do that to me?" he asked, feigning shock and holding his hands up in front of him. "Your best friend?"

"*Ex* best friend," I said, coldly. "Ex *everything*."

A glint of hurt crossed his face. "Then go ahead. Do it."

I stared at him for a moment, watching as that glint of hurt morphed into a playful challenge—those green eyes daring me to fight back—and I squeezed the trigger. The hose, which I had assumed would be set to a gentle spray setting, had actually been left on jet stream. A powerful blast of water shot out of the nozzle, hitting him square in the crotch. I kept the stream going for a few seconds, then I dropped the hose and ran.

A blast of ice-cold water hit me square in the back, soaking through three layers of clothing. I ran for the rope ladder dangling from the tree house at the edge of the yard. Trusting that it wasn't completely rotted, I pulled myself up—but not before taking another spray of water to the back of the head—until I was safely inside. I backed into a corner as Kit's head popped up a moment later.

"Truce!" I said, holding up my hands and shivering, not sure how far the garden hose could actually reach. "Remember? We had a truce!"

"I am unarmed," he announced, climbing the rest of the way in and pulling the ladder up after him.

"Sorry about that," I said, pointing to the huge wet spot on the front of his jeans.

"Are you?" he asked, taking a step toward me. "Because it looked to me like you were enjoying yourself."

"Well *yeah*," I said. "It was obviously an enjoyable moment. But, I'm also sorry because now I'm soaked, too." I took off my wet coat and sweatshirt, using the sweatshirt to pat my hair dry before flinging it into his chest. He caught it and tossed it onto a small table against the wall.

"You think it's safe to be up here?" I asked, bouncing a bit on the floorboards, suddenly noticing how new they looked. I was also suddenly aware of how alone we were up there in a tree house with the ladder pulled in. *He's a heartless jerk, Amy. Don't you forget that. A cold, heartless jerk*. So what if he was about to hand-deliver homemade scarecrows to elderly shut-ins? Even Genghis Khan must have done nice things every now and then, right? Maybe.

"It's safe," he said, running his hand along the back wall, which was a different color wood than the others. "I fixed it up a few years ago so the neighborhood kids could play in it."

I groaned as a I felt a huge chunk of my resolve go crumbling to the ground.

"What?" asked Kit.

"First, I find out that you volunteer with the old folks, and now you're telling me you fixed up a tree house for the neighborhood kids? You just—" I looked away, shaking my head. "You make it so *hard*."

He took a step toward me. "I make what hard?"

"Convincing myself that you're this cold, heartless jerk," I said honestly, looking up at him and shaking my head. "Convincing myself to hate you."

"So, you don't hate me?"

"I've been gone for ten years," I said, my chest tightening. "I moved to another state...I almost *married* another guy...I came back here to find that you want to kick out my grandpa and sell my house...and yet—" Tears welled up in my eyes. "I still love you."

"I still love you, too," he said gently, and my knees went weak at the sound of those words. "So, tell me...what are the chances of us making this work?"

"Not good," I said, walking over to the window and staring out into the branches. I'd always dreamed of a time when Kit and I might exchange those words again. Too bad reality wasn't going to have my dream ending.

"Not good like one in a hundred?" he asked, coming up beside me. I looked over to find that playful gleam back in his eyes.

"More like one in a million," I said, playing along. I'd lost count of how many times we'd watched *Dumb and Dumber* back in high school.

He nudged me with his elbow. "So, you're telling me there's a chance?"

Unable to resist the charms of Kit Parker channeling Lloyd Christmas, I nudged him back. Before I knew it, my arms were around his neck, and he was kissing me as we backed in the direction of the table and chair. Kit sank down and pulled me onto his cold, wet lap.

"This is disgusting," I murmured as we went back to kissing.

"Totally gross," he murmured back, twisting his fingers through my damp hair.

After a while, I pulled away and rested my forehead against his cheek.

"You may not hate me," he said, "but I know you're still mad at me."

"Good. I was afraid I might not be getting my point across." I kissed him lightly down the side of his neck.

"You know, I would always have wanted to buy this house." He shifted to look at me. "Unless you can go back in time and keep my mom from making that journal, this was always going to be my end game. Whether you left Tom alone up here, or whether your whole family had stayed, it wouldn't have made any difference."

"Maybe," I said, unconvinced.

"I've been thinking a lot these past few days," he said, tucking a piece of hair behind my ear, studying my face. "About how I don't want to lose you again."

I waited for him to continue, curious as to what he was about to say next.

"A few weeks ago," he said, "I thought everything was falling into place for me to finally make the inn happen. But then you showed up on the side of that highway, and now I realize that maybe I was wrong. Maybe what was really falling into place, was the chance for us to finally be together. The inn, the renovations, the money, it's all so uncertain. Maybe what I should be focusing on is the one thing I am certain about...you."

My heart swelled at the hope his words gave me while my stomach knotted at the thought of Josie telling me that she'd love to invest in the inn. The money for the renovations wasn't *quite* as uncertain as he thought...

"Instead of changing the house we grew up in," he continued before I could speak, "maybe I should be asking you to live in it with me. I know my mom wouldn't have wanted her inn at the expense of losing you. Neither do I. Maybe the special thing about this house, is that it was always meant to be ours."

I practically melted into him, his words like the "Hallelujah Chorus" to my ears. *Finally*. Finally, he'd come around to seeing this entire debacle from my perspective. I pulled him close and kissed him again.

"I think," I said, breaking away and looking deeply into those green eyes, "that we can definitely make this work."

CHAPTER 26

The following week was a happy blur of making up for lost time. Kit and I spent every free moment we had together, and at the end of the week, I booked us on a last-minute getaway to Lake Winnipesaukee. With most of the hotels and motels in the area booked due to fall foliage, the only reservation I could find was at a small bed-and-breakfast in Meredith. I had a few nagging doubts about taking Kit to a place that might remind him of what he'd decided to give up, but I booked it anyway. I mean, he hadn't *really* given anything up, had he? Nobody had forced him into making this decision. He was simply letting go of an idea he'd been toying with, back when he thought that he was never going to see me again. Now that I was here, it was only natural that some of those plans would need to change. It was what he wanted. It was what Rebecca would have wanted. He'd said it himself.

It wasn't until we'd pulled into the driveway of the B&B that I realized booking this place was, perhaps, not *the most* amazing decision I'd ever made in my life. The similarities to our house in Autumnboro were striking—starting with the adorable sign, dangling from two chains, straight out of the pages of Rebecca's journal. Kit looked as if he'd been stabbed in the chest as I dragged him inside, past the scarecrows and pumpkins strewn around the front porch, and over to the check-in desk.

Thankfully, the woman behind the desk didn't look anything like Rebecca, but Kit still listened to her attentively, taking it all in. *Room key. Homemade pumpkin pie. Breakfast at seven. Enjoy your stay!* I had a knot in my stomach as I sensed all the what-ifs and what-could've-beens whizzing around in his head. When she'd finally finished with her spiel, I hurried Kit through the cozy lobby, which looked eerily like Grandpa's living room—even down to the antique photographs of Lake Winnipesaukee on the walls—and up the stairs to our room.

Aside from a slightly bumpy start, and the occasional far-off look on Kit's face every time we entered or exited the B&B, we had a pretty amazing couple of days. Between the lazy mornings, scenic hikes, and romantic dinners, it was the happiest weekend of my life. Sunday evening, I called my mother to let her know that Kit and I were back together and that I was planning to stay in Autumnboro. She was surprised at how quickly it had all happened, although the fact that I would be taking on responsibility for Grandpa was enough to garner her full approval and support. She even offered to pack up my things and put my condo on the market.

It was now Monday morning, I was back home, and Grandpa was acting fishy.

At first, I thought it was because the Medi-Magic 3000 had gone off at Led Zeppelin-level volume while he was standing directly in front of it. But even after he'd yanked its plug out of the wall and told it to take a hike, he still seemed on edge. As I prepared our breakfast in the kitchen, he kept glancing up at the clock.

"You okay?" I asked, buttering a slice of toast.

"Sure, sure," he mumbled, standing up and leaving the room. He walked all the way to the living room window, pushed the curtains aside, and peered out. "But you might want to come and have a look at this."

"If it's those two guys holding hands again, I already explained that to you."

"It's not *that*. Just...get over here."

I put down the toast and joined him at the living-room window. Across the street on the common, the word "PROM" had been spelled out in pumpkins. Enormous orange letters stretched from the children's playground all the way to the gazebo. At the end of the word was an equally enormous orange question mark. It was really quite impressive.

"Aw, that's so sweet," I said, patting Grandpa on the shoulder. "Some high school kid must have been out there all night setting that up."

High school boys dreaming up creative ways to ask girls to the prom wasn't a thing back when I was in school. Thank God. At least when Kit had refused to take me to ours, it wasn't amidst all my friends receiving elaborate and romantic "promposals." That would've killed me, for sure. I walked back into the kitchen, wondering who the lucky neighborhood girl was. Wondering if she already had a dress picked out like I had...or if she'd had no intention of going and would have to run out and quickly find one. Or maybe she'd say no. Maybe she'd tell the poor guy that she already had a date, or that she only thought of him as a friend, and he'd be stuck hauling two hundred pumpkins back home in his Prius with nothing to show for it.

You realize the prom isn't held in fall, right? a small voice whispered in the back of my head, as I went back to buttering toast. Okay, sure. The timing on this promposal was a bit weird. But in this town, if you wanted to be the first person to spell out the word PROM in pumpkins, you needed to act fast. Whoever this kid was, he was going to have his prom date locked down well before Halloween. Good for him. I was just about to pour myself some coffee when a text buzzed on my phone. Kit.

Come outside. Followed by a wink emoji.

I smiled. He must've noticed the pumpkins, too, and wanted to watch the proposal outside with me. I hadn't realized he was such a romantic.

"I'll be right back," I said to Grandpa, grabbing my coat and taking off down the stairs.

My breath caught in my throat as I stepped onto the front porch and found Kit standing in the middle of the lawn, dressed in a black tuxedo. In his hand was a single red rose. I'd never in my life seen him so dressed up...all polished, and dashing, and dreamy. And then there was me, wearing my Losers' Club sweatshirt and pajama pants. I ran a hand pointlessly through my hair, my heart pounding.

"You got my message?" he asked, walking closer to the porch.

"The text?" I joked, holding up my phone. He slowly shook his head from side to side.

"Try again."

I walked down the porch steps to meet him on the grass, not caring that my pink fuzzy slippers were getting soaked through with dew, and swallowed past the lump in my throat. Those pumpkins were for *me*? That didn't make any sense. I reached up and fiddled with his lapel. "It was a bit subtle, but yeah. I saw it."

He smiled and handed me the rose. When he started to get down on one knee, I thought I was going to pass out. Was this an *actual* proposal? Did I have time to change out of my jammies? I relaxed a bit when he realized how wet the grass was and stood back up.

"Amy Evangeline Fox," he said, "will you go to the prom with me?"

"That sounds lovely." I laughed as tears came to my eyes. "Except for the fact that we're nearly thirty. And it's October."

"Minor details." He pulled a folded piece of paper from his

jacket pocket and handed it to me. I eyed him suspiciously as I unfolded it.

You are cordially invited to the
  Autumnboro Senior Center's
  "Senior Prom"
  Saturday October 27th

"The senior prom," I muttered, and now the tears were really starting to flow. "You're taking me to the *senior* senior prom?"

"It's about time, don't you think?"

"How did you even set all of this up?" I asked, flinging my arms around his neck, holding him tightly. "We came back so late last night!"

"Riley made a few trips to the pumpkin patch for me yesterday, while we were away. More than a few, actually. I promised to let him plan my funeral in return."

I laughed. "That's incredibly sweet and morbid of him. But I love it. All of it. This is amazing." I ran my hand down his cheek. "You're amazing."

"The funny thing," he said, squeezing my hand, "is that I'd been planning this senior center event for months. Long before I had any idea you were coming back. I was right when I said that everything was falling into place for us."

"I love you," I said, beaming up at him. Never meaning three words more in my life.

"Should I take that as a yes, then?" he asked. "Because I can return the tux early, if not. Save a few bucks."

"Don't you *ever* return this tux," I said, running my eyes down the full length of his body, and then back up to his face. "That was definitely a yes. Kit Parker, I would love to go to the prom with you."

And even though it was ten years later than planned, those words still sounded as sweet as I'd always imagined.

* * *

THE SENIOR PROM was held in the auditorium of Town Hall, which was only two days away from being transformed into a massive haunted house. Cardboard boxes overflowing with skulls and zombie parts had been pushed into a corner, and a row of Styrofoam gravestones was lined up against the back wall. Twinkle lights and black-and-white streamers had been strung all around the room, the overhead lights had been turned down to a moderate dimness, and old-time music was playing at a reasonable volume.

"This is exactly how I always imagined our prom." I smiled up at Kit as we walked into the auditorium. An elderly couple shuffled past, shouting to each other about hearing aids. "It's perfect."

I found a table with Grandpa and Maggie while Kit went off to get us some drinks. Once Maggie had found out that I was staying in Autumnboro, and not plotting to snatch Grandpa out of her life, she turned out to be a much nicer person than I'd thought. She'd even come prom dress shopping with Josie and me, and looked beautiful in the silver sequined shift dress we helped pick out. For myself, I'd chosen a black, floor-length gown with a halter neck and an open back.

I watched Kit as he walked toward the makeshift bar, all handsome and tuxedoed, getting sidetracked by pretty much everybody. They all wanted to shake his hand and thank him for arranging the evening. Susan Blake was there, too, wearing a crimson cocktail dress with autumn leaves woven into her hair, which she'd twisted up into a neat bun. She still refused to acknowledge my existence, but she looked lovely.

Later on in the evening, after I was worn out from dancing, I plunked down at the table beside Grandpa. Kit had wandered off to deal with a sound system issue, and Maggie was sitting at another table chatting with Barbara and Walter.

"Having a good time?" I asked. He looked adorable in his tux with the red rose boutonnière that Josie had surprised him with.

"You bet," he said. "You?"

"The best."

He smiled. "Good. I'm glad everything's finally working out for you two."

"So am I," I said. "I never could have imagined this. Not even a month ago."

"You're happy then?"

"Of course."

"And Osiris, he's a distant memory?"

"*Orion.*" I laughed. "And yes, Grandpa. He is a distant turd of a memory."

"Good. Now, tell me about that one." He jerked his thumb in the general direction of Kit. "Is he happy, too?"

"Of course," I said, my defenses prickling. "I mean, I think so. Why would you say it like that?"

He didn't immediately respond, and a few seconds of silence passed while I strangled a paper napkin between my hands.

"You know," he said at last, "I was wrong when I told you that the house was my last connection to your grandmother. My biggest connection to her is sitting right here next to me. I see her face every time I look at you." He smiled at me, and I fought to keep my composure. "Having you, and any grandchildren you might decide to bless me with, nearby," he continued, "is all I need to keep her memory alive, darling. Not some drafty old house. That house has big things in store for it. Much bigger things than me."

"Grandpa—" I started.

"I want your mother to sell," he interrupted, looking at me sternly. "It's the right time, and it's for the right reason. Besides, I don't want any expensive stair lifts or surveillance cameras or any of that foolish business."

"Surveillance cameras?"

"I found the pamphlets in the kitchen drawer, Amy. I'm not dense."

I bit my lip and shrank down in my seat.

"All I ask," he continued, "is that wherever you move, you set aside a small place for me. Modest accommodations. A broom closet, or a room beneath the stairs, like that Potter kid. I don't need much."

"I think we could do a bit better than that," I said, brushing a tear from my cheek. "But are you sure about this? I mean, the house has been in our family for *years*."

"And it still will be," he said, meeting my eyes. "I have faith in the two of you."

"But—"

"No buts. You left me up here for a long time, and I know you feel guilty about that. But you came back when I needed you, no questions asked. My heart," he clasped a hand to his chest, "is full." At the sight of Grandpa grabbing his chest, the paramedic hanging out by the punch bowl started to rush over. Grandpa waved him away. "So, tell me, darling...do we have a deal?"

Before I could answer, we were interrupted by a massive screech of feedback. The room went silent as Kit walked out onto the dance floor, microphone in hand. "Amy Fox to the dance floor," he said. "Amy...Fox...to the dance floor."

The music changed from some doo-woppy fifties tune to "Hey There Delilah," which had been our original high school prom song. Or so I'd heard. Feeling a bit wobbly, and unsure of when my life had turned from a horror novel into a fairy tale, I stood up and smoothed out my dress. Who was I kidding? I knew exactly when it had happened. It wasn't the moment that Kit stepped out of a tow truck and back into my life...although, that was close. It was the moment that Grandpa stepped on the gas instead of the brake and drove through the window of a Dunkin' Donuts.

Before heading out onto the dance floor to dance at the prom with the love of my life, I leaned down and whispered into Grandpa's ear. "It's a deal."

CHAPTER 27

Four nights later, we were back at Town Hall.

Kit had called in a favor with the town clerk—the most famous person he'd ever towed until I'd come sputtering into town—and arranged for an emergency town meeting. Unfortunately, the only night she could squeeze us in was on Halloween, and the only time she had available was the hour before the Town Hall haunted house was set to open. Pretty much all of Autumnboro shut down early on Halloween night, which explained why I was pacing the auditorium dressed like the Corpse Bride. As soon as we were finished, Josie and I needed to get over to the store to start handing out candy to trick-or-treaters.

Kit and I had managed to squeeze several dozen chairs in between rows of gravestones, careful not to step on the fog machines and zombie parts that had been carefully laid out. As I paced the room, flipping through my note cards and rehearsing exactly what I was planning to say, I tripped over a skeleton and fell to my knees. I stood up, activating a bloodcurdling shriek from the dangling ghoul I'd backed into, and finally just took a seat at the front of the room.

"You'll be fine," said Kit, pulling up a chair next to me. He was dressed as Victor Van Dort, the Corpse Bride's love interest, and he looked fantastic. His hair had been dyed jet black, and his face was covered in pale white powder. My stomach, awash with nerves, allowed in a little flutter of excitement as I looked into his handsome face. I could have delayed this town meeting until after Halloween when we wouldn't have been dressed like fools...but I didn't want to wait a minute longer. It had to be tonight.

At precisely four o'clock, a mumbling stream of townspeople began filing into the auditorium. Like me, many of them were already in costume. Jackie Braeburn and her husband led the way, dressed as bacon and eggs, and behind them was Moose in a bulging green Hulk costume. The crew from the Shaky Maple were dressed as cups of coffee and assorted pastries, and the Autumnboro Ballers came in dressed as a bowling team from the 1980s. Unless it was just their regular bowling night. I wasn't totally sure.

Loads of people I didn't know continued coming in, all curious to find out what this meeting was about. Many of them were probably going to leave here disappointed, but that was okay. I smiled at the sight of Josie, Maggie, Grandpa, and Riley as they came through the door dressed as a colorful group of Pokémon. Following behind them were two people in Barack and Michelle Obama masks. I waved to Michelle, and she waved back. Everything was on track.

As soon as everybody had found a seat, I stepped up to the podium.

"Look who it is!" shouted a voice from the back. "What'd you do, call us all here to rip us apart some more?"

"Maybe she's got a movie deal and needs us to sign waivers!" shouted somebody else. My stomach knotted as I waited for all the angry murmurs of agreement to die down.

"I appreciate all of you coming here tonight," I said into the microphone. "I know that it's a busy night here in Autumnboro, but this won't take long." I picked up my note cards just as the dangling ghoul let out another bloodcurdling shriek, making me drop them all on the floor.

"Mr. Woodbury, if you wouldn't mind stepping away from the ghoul?" I motioned for the elderly man to take a few steps to his right. "There. Perfect. Okay." I picked up my note cards, cleared my throat, and looked at Kit in the front row. He gave me a thumbs-up.

"As many of you know, I wrote some books that were based on this town and on the people in it." I glanced around the room at all the judgmental faces, catching the eye of Barbara Cortland. She was wearing Groucho glasses and a floppy beach hat, and she gave me a curt but encouraging nod. I took a deep breath and went on. "I came here tonight not only to apologize, but to try to explain. When I wrote those books, I'd been away from this town for quite a few years. I'd left the love of my life behind," I glanced up at Kit, "and that didn't leave me in a very good place."

I paused as I shuffled the note cards nervously around in my hands. "When I wrote those books," I continued, "it was with a sour grapes mentality. An *if I can't be there, then I'm going to pretend that it was all terrible* sort of attitude. But that was only a defense mechanism. A cowardly bit of self-preservation. Deep down, I have always loved this town. I *still* love this town. When I was in Pennsylvania, I had a huge fall-themed wedding planned because I could never quite shake this place. And, it seems that I couldn't shake any of you, either."

I looked again around the room, to find several of the angry faces starting to soften.

"This town full of colorful, unique characters kept right on living inside my head, no matter how long I was away. And eventually, I decided that I didn't want to keep you all to myself anymore." I laid my note cards down on the podium and focused my attention on the eyes of the audience.

"So yes, I may have portrayed Susan, over there, as the town gossip." I motioned to Susan who, for the first time in weeks, looked me hesitantly in the eye. "And I'm sorry for that. But if it weren't for Susan's love of chitchat, would Arthur and Bonnie McShane have ever gotten married?" I motioned to the cute couple sitting across the aisle. "Neither one knew that the other had a crush on them until Susan came along and blabbed it all over town!"

Several people nodded in agreement, including Susan.

"And yes, I may have portrayed Donnie, over there, as a crook, who would sell his soul to the devil." I looked to Donnie, who was apparently filming me with his iPhone. "And I'm sorry for that, too. But, if I remember correctly, after he overcharged my father for brake pads, he also made an extremely generous donation to the food bank." Donnie lowered his phone and nodded humbly as everybody turned to look at him.

"And Moose, I *love* that you drove under a moose. That doesn't make you a fool like police officer Buck. It makes you a legend! Most people *die* when they hit a moose, Moose. But you...you're a survivor."

Moose's expression was unreadable, so I moved on to Jackie.

"And Jackie. Sure, the Striped Blueberry gave everybody food poisoning. But, do you know what else that tacky, straight-out-of-the-eighties diner gave everybody in the town of Fallsburg? A place to gather with friends and family. And if they didn't have any friends or family, it gave them a place where they could go and never have to feel alone. A place where there was always an open seat at the counter and a kind person behind it who was always happy to talk."

Everybody turned to smile at Jackie whose face was turning pink inside her bacon costume.

"So, for all of you, whatever I may have written, just know that it was written out of fondness, and affection, and love." I placed one hand over my heart. "Even if I had a warped and twisted way of showing it, I have the greatest respect for each and every one of you. Now, if you'll all take a moment to check beneath your seats," I waited while everybody retrieved the binder-clipped packet of papers I'd placed underneath, "you'll find the first half of my latest novel."

I felt a bit like Oprah. Only, instead of finding a free diamond watch or tickets for an African safari, they were discovering an unedited first draft of a book by an author they hated. "I think that if you give it a chance, you'll find some of the character arcs quite interesting. And I hope, after reading, that you'll find it in your hearts to forgive me."

There was a moment of quiet as everybody started flipping through the pages. A moment later, they all stood up to leave.

"Wait!" I shouted into the microphone. "I have one more thing to say!" With a collective groan, they sat back down. I took a deep breath. "Kit Parker, could you please come up here?"

Looking confused, he rose from his seat and joined me at the podium. I motioned to Michelle Obama, who removed her mask.

"Mrs. Fox?" asked Kit, squinting.

"Hello, Kit," said Mom. She joined us at the podium, carrying a manila envelope, and gave him a hug. The person in the Barack mask followed her, pulling it off as he faced the audience.

"Is that Isaac Mizrahi?" called out Moose. Isaac waved.

"He wanted to see the quaint little town I'd grown up in," said Mom, looking at me with a shrug. "So I brought him along."

"Anyway," I said, turning back to Kit. "I love you. And I can't wait to start my new life with you here in this town. But, before we can do that, there's one more thing that we need to settle."

Mom opened the manila envelope and shook out a thick stack of documents, handing them to Kit. He stared at the top page for a moment, his eyes widening.

"The deed to the house," he said, softly.

"We're ready to sign when you are," said Mom. "My father, he had the final word."

Grandpa nodded to us from the front row.

"I...I don't know what to say," said Kit. "I thought—"

"There is a tiny bit more," I cut in. "Josie here, she wants to invest. So, you can start on the renovations as soon as you'd like. The Autumnboro Inn is a go."

Josie gave me a double thumbs-up, beaming at us from her seat beside Grandpa.

"Are you sure about this?" asked Kit, turning to me. His eyes had lit up in a way I hadn't seen in years, making my heart squeeze with joy. *Now* everything had fallen into place. Now everything was right.

"I'm sure."

I reached up and wrapped my arms around his neck. Then I kissed him, right there, in front of Mom, and Grandpa, and Isaac Mizrahi. I kissed him, with all of my heart, in front of the entire crazy town.

* * *

I walked to Pumpkin Everything the next morning to find all the pumpkin merchandise removed from the window of The Plaid Apple. The senior center shuttle drove past with a friendly toot and a wave from Susan. Moose, who was across the street sweeping the steps of the mini mart, looked up and gave me a tip of his Red Sox cap. When I returned home later in the day, I found my car parked in the driveway. It had been washed and detailed, and a note had been taped to the dashboard. In the center of the note were just two words, but those two words meant everything to me.

Welcome Home.

ONE YEAR LATER....

I closed my laptop and stretched.

I'd been writing for two hours straight and was in desperate need of a bathroom break and some coffee. Leaving the turret, I ran downstairs into what used to be Kit and Riley's apartment. It was now a reception area with a check-in desk, fireplace, comfortable chairs, and Grandpa's collection of New Hampshire memorabilia on display just about everywhere. His Concord coach had a special case of its own by the front window, and just below the ceiling a model train chugged its way around the entire first floor. I smiled at the framed photograph of Rebecca, Kit, and Riley that was hanging near the bottom of the stairs, before heading through the dining room and into the kitchen.

"Hey there," said Kit. He stopped unpacking boxes of kitchen supplies long enough to kiss me. "How's the writing going?"

"Book two, almost complete," I said, taking a seat at the island. "I never thought I'd say those words again."

While the rest of the house had undergone renovations—I'd said a teary goodbye to the initials at the back of my closet—the turret had been preserved. It had been walled off, with a locking door, and a sign that read *Private.* The turret was now my office, the place where I finally got my writing mojo back, and the one piece of this house that would always be mine.

The inn wasn't quite ready to open yet, and probably wouldn't be until Christmas. It was a shame to miss out on opening in time for autumn, but it had been a bit of a crazy year...and we had plenty more autumns ahead.

Over the summer, Kit and I were married at the summit of Loon Mountain. After exchanging vows, we were whisked by gondola back down to the lodge where our wedding reception awaited. Our wedding gift from my parents was the down payment on a small house not far from the inn with a cozy in-law apartment for Grandpa. Mom said it was the least she could do to contribute to his well-being, before heading back to her glamorous life in Pennsylvania.

Isaac Mizrahi could not make the wedding but sent his regards.

Josie continued working at Pumpkin Everything, bringing new life and fresh energy to the store. So when she eventually offered to buy it, Grandpa happily agreed. His only condition was that he still be allowed to work there, part-time, lest his mind turn to mush and we ship him off to Winter's Eve. Josie happily agreed.

Riley still works at Goldwyn & Hays and found himself a nice apartment just over the town line in Summerboro. I've been keeping my fingers crossed that he, too, will find his happily ever after.

"Ready for a break?" I asked. It was a beautiful fall day, perfect for a walk around the common.

"Let's blow this popsicle stand." Kit grabbed the coffeepot off the burner and filled up two travel mugs. As we walked through the reception area and onto the front porch, I took a deep inhale of my coffee.

"Pumpkin spice," I said savoring the rich scent. "Yum."

As I took a sip, Kit grabbed my hand and we walked down the steps of The Autumnboro Inn.

AFTERWORD

Thank you so much for reading *Pumpkin Everything*. As a child, I spent many summers with my family in the White Mountains of New Hampshire. The Flume is still one of my most favorite places in the world, I'm still afraid of the Wolfman at Clark's Trading Post, and I will always get teary-eyed when I think about the Old Man of the Mountain, gone in the night. I hope you enjoyed reading about Amy, Kit and their beautiful home as much as I enjoyed writing about them.

If *Pumpkin Everything* helped get you into the fall spirit, please consider leaving a review on Amazon.com. Reviews mean the world to authors and are very much appreciated. Kind of like a pumpkin spice latte on a brisk autumn day.

If you're into that sort of thing.

ABOUT THE AUTHOR

Beth Labonte received a B.A. in Sociology from the University of Massachusetts Amherst. She worked as an administrative assistant for fourteen years, turning to writing as her creative outlet in an excruciatingly mundane corporate world. Beth now writes full-time and resides in Massachusetts.

SNEAK PEEK

Turn the page for a peek at Josie's story:

Maple Sugar Crush

MAPLE SUGAR CRUSH

Last Thanksgiving

"I'm just so excited about the inn!" I said, scooping mashed potatoes onto my plate and passing the bowl along to my sister. "I have so many ideas! I'm thinking wind spinners for the front lawn! They have some amazing ones on QVC right now, so I went ahead and ordered ten. If Kit and Amy don't want them, I'll just donate them, well...somewhere! The funeral home could always use some brightening up! Oh, and you should really see the drawings that Kit's mother did in her journal. They're *so* gorgeous. Amy is so lucky she gets to work there—part-time, of course, since she's still writing her books. She's the *best* author. I'm hoping they let me work there too, even though I'm already so busy at Pumpkin Everything, and—"

I looked across the table at my mother, whose face had frozen into a semi-interested half-smile. I do tend to ramble. Or perhaps she'd gone in for a bit of pre-Thanksgiving Botox.

"Sorry." I shrugged. "It's just been a long time since I've had something to look forward to."

"What I don't understand, is why you still want to work at all?" asked Mom. "All this talk about working at the inn, working at the store. Why not just relax? You could be living down here with us, by the ocean, where it doesn't always smell like pumpkins and manure. You could buy a yacht!"

"Autumnboro doesn't smell like manure, Mom. And you know I'm not crazy about boats. Way too many ways to drown. Besides, I'm only thirty. I'd go out of my mind if I retired now."

I glanced across the table at my father, because even in his fifties I knew he probably felt the same way. I often think he'd have been happier had I never won all this money. All this money being the four hundred and fifty-eight million-dollar Powerball jackpot I'd hit five years ago. I know, right? Go ahead and pick yourself up off the floor. I sure had to when *I* found out.

"I'm happy for you, Josie," said my sister, Meg, giving my hand a squeeze. "It's nice that you've made a home for yourself in Autumnboro. And found such good friends."

"Yeah, it must be *so* tough being a multi-millionaire," said my cousin, Audrey, glopping a spoonful of potatoes onto her plate. "I feel *so* bad for you." She passed the bowl to her husband, Randy, who snorted in agreement.

"Tell us, Josie," said my uncle, Burt, from the other end of the table, "have you booked a seat on that spaceship to Mars yet?" He let out a loud guffaw, clearly pleased with his cleverness. He made that same joke every time he saw me.

"Not yet," I said, rolling my eyes and taking a sip of wine. "But I'm happy to pay for your trip, Uncle Burt. I hear it's a one-way."

"You'd better take her up on that," said my aunt, Carla, pointing a fork in her husband's direction. "That's the most generous she's been with any of us."

"That is *not* true!" said Dad, his own fork clattering to his plate as he glared down the table at his sister. "Josie has been very generous with all of us! It's not her fault if you people don't know how to manage your finances." He loosened his collar and went back to eating.

This was typical.

I'd already spent the greater part of the day dodging requests for money. Everywhere I turned, another relation seemed to pop out of the woodwork with their hand out. Not to be one of those *winning the lottery ruined my life* types, but family get-togethers have become a major source of anxiety. It's just a fact. My money, and what I've been doing with it, is pretty much all we ever talk about. They think I'm wasting it. The funny thing is that I mostly try to do *good* things with my money, rather than blowing it on the frivolous materialistic sort of junk they would choose.

After I'd won, I'd taken care of my immediate family first. I bought Meg and her husband, Dave, a nice house up in Kennebunkport, and set up college funds for my two nieces. Then I made sure they quit their jobs and pursued their dream of opening up a coffee shop, which they'd kindly named Josie Beans.

I bought my parents and my grandmother an oceanfront home on Cape Cod—where we were now enjoying Thanksgiving dinner—and pushed them into a relatively early retirement. Mom quit her office manager job of thirty years, and gleefully leaped into a life of leisure. She made friends with all the neighborhood ladies, took up golf, and sought out every anti-aging potion money could buy. I'd introduced her to QVC—along with the fact that Amy's mother was a host—which may have been a mistake, but there was no stopping her now. Dad, who maybe hadn't been quite ready to retire from teaching, seemed bored. He wasn't interested in shopping or golf. He'd taken to walking up and down the beach with a beat-up metal detector he'd found at a local flea market. Granny lives in the in-law apartment and has been having trouble with her memory these past few years.

Having her around to care for might be the only thing still grounding my mother to reality.

As for the extended family, I'd followed the advice of my financial planner by paying off their debts and gifting them with enough money that—had they invested it wisely—would have taken care of them for life. I looked over at Uncle Burt, who was picking his teeth with the wishbone. Not all of them had been so wise.

"She could always be slightly *more* generous, couldn't she?" asked Audrey. "It's not like she's in danger of ever running out of money."

"How much did you win, dear?" asked Granny, leaning forward with interest, as if I'd hit for twenty bucks on a scratch ticket. No matter how much the family went on about it, Granny never managed to remember. The one time I refreshed her memory, she had to be taken to the emergency room with heart palpitations, so I've been playing it down ever since.

"That's not important, Granny. More wine?" I refilled her glass with cranberry juice.

"What are you down to now?" asked Audrey. "Four hundred and fifty-seven mil?" Granny's eyes widened and she clutched at her necklace.

"She's *joking*," I said, shooting Audrey a look. "Weren't you?"

"Of course," said Audrey, giving Granny a patronizing smile. "I was totally kidding. It's all one…big…funny…joke." She eyed me as she annunciated the last four words.

"What do you even do with it, anyway?" asked Randy. "You don't travel, you don't have a boyfriend…" He ticked each item off on his beefy fingers. As if *he* had any right to comment on my love life. Audrey's no peach, but how he even ended up with *her* is beyond me.

"I donate to countless charities," I said, placing one hand on my chest. "I just invested in my friend's inn! Haven't you been listening at all?"

"And here *we* are, struggling to pay for groceries each week," said Audrey, shaking her head and looking around the table for sympathy.

"I have five dollars in my purse, dear," said Granny, rewarding her with an understanding frown. "I'll give it to you after dinner. But you have to promise to split it with your brother."

"Granny, keep your money." I turned back to Audrey and Randy. "I gave you two *plenty*," I hissed, out of Granny's range of hearing. "How can you possibly not be able to pay for *groceries*?"

"Speaking of being thirty, Josie," interrupted Mom, apropos of nothing. "Have you met any men up there in New Hampshire?" She talked about New Hampshire as if it were a faraway land, even though we'd lived there most of our lives. It was only two years ago that my parents moved from Nashua to Cape Cod, and I decided to start over fresh in Autumnboro.

"Of course, I've met some *men*," I said, grateful for the change of subject. Even if the subject was still me, at least it wasn't about my money. "There's Kit and Riley. Moose and Donnie. And Tom, of course. He's the best."

"Oh," said Mom, her face lighting up. She gripped the edge of the table with perfectly polished, burgundy nails. "Who's this Tom?"

"Amy's grandpa. He owns Pumpkin Everything, remember? Drove his Jeep through the front of Dunkin Donuts? That's why Amy had to come home in the first place, to make sure he didn't get moved into assisted living and—"

"Never mind," groaned Mom, resting her forehead in her palm and holding the other hand up in the air. "I remember. For a minute I thought maybe Tom was *your* age."

"I wish. He has a girlfriend, anyway. Maggie. She used to be married to Peter Hays, who co-owned the funeral home. She still works there part-time."

"Of course, she does," mumbled Mom, running her fingers

through her dyed blonde bob. "Meg, the wine please." My sister passed her the bottle and Mom refilled her glass.

"The turkey was delicious, by the way," said Dad. "You did a wonderful job, Josie. As usual."

"Here, here!" said Meg, clinking my wine glass.

"The Winchesters hired a chef this year, did I tell you?" said Mom. "Michelin starred."

"Which means they cooked up some sort of frou-frou tofurkey nonsense," said Dad. "I'll take Josie's regular cooking any day. She's *dad*-starred."

"Thanks, Dad" I said, blinking back a few tears. His jokes were lame, but sweet. Exactly what you needed from a dad on Thanksgiving.

The first Thanksgiving after I'd won the lottery, Mom wanted to hire a professional chef to cook us dinner. I was so uncomfortable with the thought of us lounging around like kings, waiting to be served, that I told Mom if she didn't want to cook anymore, I'd be happy to do it. She didn't put up much of a fight, and I've been doing it ever since.

Once dinner was over, I went into the kitchen to put on a pot of coffee and prepare for dessert. I may have gone a little overboard with the desserts. I've always liked to support Autumnboro's small businesses, so this year I ordered pies from both The Plaid Apple and The Shaky Maple. But then, some high school kids stopped by the store selling pies to support the marching band, so I'd ordered a few from them, as well. Then some *more* kids had come by, selling pies to support the football team, and when I tried to tell them I'd already ordered from the marching band, they looked seriously offended and said, "We have literally nothing to do with each other," and also, "Didn't you win the lottery?" So, I ordered five more.

Then there was the flyer somebody left in my mailbox, saying that Grayson's Turkey Farm was donating half of their Thanksgiving pie proceeds to the animal shelter, so I went ahead and ordered twenty from them. *Twenty.* I know. I ended up giving some away around town, and I left a few in the freezer at home, but even so…it's a good thing Mom and Dad's new house came with a big refrigerator.

I was half inside said refrigerator, trying to extricate the pie boxes, when the doorbell rang.

"Josie!" called Mom. "Could you come out here, please?"

I took a step back, closed the refrigerator doors, and took a deep breath. Some distant relative must have decided to stop by to beg me for money. This was nothing new, but I still hated it. I walked toward the living room, my palms starting to sweat as I rehearsed in my head how I was going to tactfully say no. Maybe if things hadn't gone so wrong for me so early on, I'd still be handing out cash left and right. But people lie, and people take advantage, and I've learned the hard way that sometimes I just have to say no. I walked into the living room to find Mom standing in front of the couch surrounded by three floppy-haired men. They were all various shades of blond and tan, dressed in khaki pants and identical black pea coats.

"Josie, this is Quinn, Dylan, and Brady. They've come by for dessert!"

"Oh," I said, nodding around at the three of them. "Hello. Are we… related?" I glanced at Mom for assistance. I'd never heard of there being a Quinn, Dylan, or Brady in the family, but you never did know. Like I said, they popped out of the woodwork.

Mom laughed and ran her fingers through her hair. "I certainly hope not! Boys, introduce yourselves!"

"Hey there," said Quinn, shrugging out of his coat and tossing it onto the couch. "I teach golf lessons at the club. Shelly's a real natural." He gave my mother a wink as he mimed a golf swing.

"I clean your parents' pool in the summer," said Dylan, attempting to follow Quinn's lead by miming a pool vacuum, which didn't look nearly as cool as he'd probably hoped. He tossed his coat on top of Quinn's.

Brady gave me a small wave. He seemed a bit shy. Almost as if Mom had thrown him into a sack and kidnapped him from his Thanksgiving dinner, which wasn't out of the question. She'd had a lot of free time while I was busy cooking. "I shampoo at your mom's salon."

"Very nice," I said, nodding politely as understanding sank in. "Would you three excuse us a minute?" I grabbed my mother by the elbow and marched her back into the kitchen.

"Aren't they just adorable?" she asked.

"How much have you told them about me?"

"What do you mean?"

"I mean, have you told them that I won the lottery?"

"Of course, I did. Everybody around here knows that. They certainly don't think a retired teacher and an office manager could afford a place like this!" She laughed as she leaned back against the island, sliding her hands across the granite.

"Mom," I sighed. "I've told you this before. Dating in my situation is extremely complicated. Have you already forgotten about Dean?" Just saying his name made my stomach turn over.

"Oh, please. These boys are nothing like Dean. You met Dean *online.*"

"Who'd she meet online?" asked Uncle Burt, suddenly appearing in the kitchen. He whistled when he saw the stack of pie boxes, then walked to the refrigerator and helped himself to another beer. "One of those Nigerian princes? I bet she'd give a boatload of money to *him* if he asked."

"Maybe if he asked me *nicely*," I said, turning back to my mother. "Look, it doesn't matter *where* I meet them, Mom. There are two things that I know about men: if they're not after my money from the very beginning, they're going to be after it eventually. And it doesn't help when you've gone and filled them in on all the details before they've even met me." I motioned toward the living room. "Although, Brady does seem sweet."

"Doesn't he? And he has the *gentlest* hands." She practically moaned as she pushed me back toward the door. "Go! Talk to him! He can love you for your personality *and* your money!"

"Mom, *no*," I said, turning back around and planting my feet. "I know you're trying to help, but you don't understand how hard this is. Now, I'm going to set out the desserts, and the guys are welcome to stay since I brought twenty different pies, but I will *not* be flirting with them or playing any sort of dating games. Do you understand? Promise me that you won't keep on giving them the wrong idea."

"Okay," said Mom, holding her hands in the air. "I promise."

I love my mother, but she didn't keep her promise.

By the end of dessert, she'd talked me and my money up so much that Meg had to take Granny upstairs for a nap, and I found myself declining a dinner invitation, a weekend in Nantucket, and a marriage proposal.

"I'm sorry," I said, as the guys filed glumly past me and down the porch steps. "It's not you, it's me! You all seem very sweet!" Brady was the last one out the door, and I put my hand on his arm to stop him. "By the way, my mother mentioned that she'd like you to be a bit rougher when shampooing her head. Really shake her around, if you could."

As I watched their taillights disappear down the road, I had a brief longing for the way Thanksgiving used to be. Back when I was young enough that my mother wasn't obsessed with finding me a husband, and nobody wanted anything from me other than simply being present at the table. Then a wave of guilt walloped me in the stomach, as it always did when I thought about the possibility of life having been better before I'd won the lottery.

I drove home the next morning, happy to be on my way back to my quiet life in Autumnboro, where I had my job at the store and my upcoming involvement with the inn. My life was full. So what if I didn't have a boyfriend? Nobody was meant to have it all. I'd already won Powerball, which made me luckier than nearly everybody else on Earth. It was a one in three hundred million chance.

How dare I expect anything more?

Buy Now on Amazon!

OTHER BOOKS BY BETH LABONTE

The Summer Series:

Summer at Sea

Summer at Sunset

Summer Baby

Holiday Sweet Romance:

Love Notes in Reindeer Falls

Merry Little Love Story in Reindeer Falls

Stuck on Your Heart: a short & sweet

Valentine's Day romance

Autumnboro Sweet Romance:

Pumpkin Everything

Maple Sugar Crush

More:

Down, Then Up: A Novella

You can also find Beth here:

www.facebook.com/bethlabontebooks

www.bethlabonte.com

Made in United States
North Haven, CT
05 August 2024